CHRISTMAS WITH AN ALIEN

A SCI-FI ALIEN HOLIDAY ROM COM

TANA STONE

BROADMOOR BOOKS

CHAPTER 1

Griff

"*How* ow much longer until we land?" I glanced at the Drexian pilot in front of me and tried to relax my grip on my knees. I might have spent half of my life in space, but the ships I traversed the galaxy on were considerably larger than the transport that was currently entering the atmosphere of Earth. I was unaccustomed to the bumpy ride of smaller ships, and I was not enjoying the sensations.

"We're almost there." The dark-haired alien craned his neck around to give me a grin. "The jumps were the hard part."

I nodded, doing my best not to think about the jumps through space that had shortened the trip from the Drexian station. My stomach was still in my throat from being tugged through the fabric of the universe, although I suspected it was more than the jumps making me feel unsettled. Dwelling on the true purpose of my trip and why it was so urgent would change nothing, so I brushed aside my anxiety and attempted to steady my breath.

"I thought Valorians were great sky wanderers," the Drexian co-pilot said, as he eyed me. "You don't look so good back there."

I doubted the alien knew what an ill Valorian looked like, since our skin was blue and rarely changed hues, even when we did have the urge to heave all over the pristine, black floor of a space vessel. "I am fine. I am just eager to arrive."

"Shopping, right?"

I cut my gaze to the Drexian seated next to me who had asked the question. He'd seemed friendly when we'd boarded the transport on the station's hangar bay, but I remembered that he was one of the Drexians who worked with the tribute bride program. Even now, he held a tablet in his hands as he scanned quickly through images of females.

"I don't blame you." He sighed without looking up. "This is the best time of year to shop on Earth."

I put my hand in my pocket, touching the small device that contained the reason I was visiting the human world. "I am interested in procurement. I have a list."

"I hope so if you're going to go shopping in New York City at Christmastime." The co-pilot let out a low whistle. "From what I hear, the place can be a madhouse."

I blinked at the back of his head. A madhouse? I did not wish to go to any place that contained the insane. "I do not want to visit mad houses."

"If it's your first time on Earth, you might need some help." The Drexian next to me straightened as the transport shuddered and dropped below the clouds. "I'd be happy to play tour guide for you, but I have to meet with some new tribute bride candidates. For some reason, a large number of our applicants have requested Christmas weddings, which means I don't have much time to finalize the selection process and return them to the station to be matched."

Even though I wasn't Drexian, I was familiar with their tribute bride program, where they matched human females to Drexian warriors in need of a mate, brought them to their holographically-enhanced space station, put them in fantasy suites, and then treated them to dream weddings in space. For decades, the Drexians had conducted the program with the permission of the Earth governments but not the general public, but after the program was made public—called the Reveal—Earth had adapted to the knowledge and females had been clamoring to be chosen for the program. The Drexians' success with the tribute brides was the reason I was on my way to Earth.

"Do not worry about me," I said. "I am sure I will adapt to Earth."

His dark brow lifted. "You say that because you've never been to New York the week before Christmas."

"What is a Christmas?"

The Drexians piloting the ship laughed. "Great question. None of us knew a thing about it until the tributes got together on the station to throw parties around the holiday."

"It's a religious holiday but also not religious," the male beside me said.

"And there is magic and immortality involved," the co-pilot added.

The pilot tapped the glossy console stretching in front of him. "Plus, elves who make toys for children."

I scratched my head. "Elves?" I had encountered a powerful race of elven princes on Golorren III and did not wish a repeat of that.

"Don't worry." The Drexian to my side lowered his voice. "None of the mythology is real, from what I can tell, but a large percentage of humans do participate in the lore. Do not try to challenge them on the stories, no matter how absurd they seem. Especially the young humans. That would not end well for you."

"Do not argue about Christmas," I muttered to myself.

"If you already have a list and know what you want, I might be able to help you." He produced a smaller device and rapidly tapped his fingers across the screen. "One of the last females I interviewed for the program works at a very large store in New York. You can find anything you could imagine there, and she is something called a personal shopper. I'll make an appointment for you, and she can help you get everything on your list."

"There is someone who can find me everything on my list?"

He tapped out a few more lines. "That's her job."

I shifted in my seat. "That would be helpful. Thank you, Drexian."

"Don't mention it, Valorian." He nudged me in the side. "My name is Dix."

I hesitated at the thought of unleashing my full Valorian name, which was hard to pronounce even for my own kind. "You can call me Griff."

"You're only the third Valorian I've met since our peoples became allies, but I'm glad you're joining our fight to protect the galaxy—and Earth."

"We are also grateful for the alliance." I didn't tell him why I was particularly pleased, or why I was journeying to the human home world.

It wasn't common knowledge that my kind were also compatible with the human species because most of the Valorians had little interest in the creatures who did not have our beautiful blue skin. But I'd seen enough images of human females and heard enough stories from content Drexians to be intrigued, blue skin or not.

I drew in a deep breath as the planet became visible, and we dropped rapidly toward a small island. I had not had success finding a mate among the dwindling numbers of female Valorians, but I was certain that I would find someone among the humans, especially since they were now so welcoming of aliens, thanks to the Drexians.

"It's all set." Dix put his device back in his pants pocket. "Go to the store called Saks Fifth Avenue and ask for a personal shopper named Olivia. She'll be waiting for you and ready to take care of that list."

I closed my eyes, thinking of the list that I'd made so carefully. After spending a great deal of time writing down all the qualities I wished to find in a mate, it would be a relief to show it to someone who knew exactly where to find such a female. This expedition to the human world might not be so difficult after all.

The Drexian interrupted my quiet reflection with a pat on the knee. "There are a few more things you should know about human females—just in case."

CHAPTER 2

Caroline

"*I*s it just me or are the days getting longer the closer we get to Christmas?" I ran a hand through my hair, trying not to think of the fact that I desperately needed to touch up my Buttercream Blonde roots.

"Or are the customers getting crazier?" My co-worker and friend Olivia sank into one of the beige chairs behind the shiny, copper-colored reception desk for The Fifth Avenue Club.

"Both." I leaned back in my chair and stole a glance around the modern space that led to the elite personal shopping department at the Saks Fifth Avenue flagship store in Manhattan. An array of glittery pendant lights hung overhead to create a chandelier effect and send light dancing across the polished cream tile floor. Gleaming wooden, floor-to-ceiling slats created a chic division and entrance to the appointment-only area. Everything about our place of work was stylish and understated—except for our holiday shoppers.

Since the calendar had flipped to December, our usual stream of upscale shoppers had become a deluge of frantic Upper East Side women with impossible lists and obscene budgets. Tempted by the concept of having a personally curated shopping list and customized holiday wardrobe, the ladies who lunched had kept us booked solid.

"It's not that I don't appreciate you getting me this job, Liv." I slid my feet from my black heels under the desk and sighed as my toes were released from their pointy prisons. "But you never mentioned what it was like at the holidays."

"Didn't I?" Olivia pulled up her dark hair into a high ponytail, whipped it into a surprisingly tidy bun, and gave a half shrug. "Are you sure this isn't a general bah humbug?"

"Me?"

She choked back a laugh. "You don't seem to be a big fan of Christmas, Caroline."

"I don't dislike Christmas, but I'm not crazy about all the commercial hype. Holiday decor goes up before Halloween candy has even been opened, and then it's just a mad rush of buying things. If you ask me, the spirit of Christmas gets lost in the shuffle."

Olivia made a show of looking around us, even though for the first time since the store's doors had opened, we were alone. "Don't let the bosses hear you. Your job kind of revolves around people buying things."

"I know, I know. Usually it doesn't get to me, but after customizing a gift list for a seven-year-old that included the latest iPhone and a diamond bracelet, I feel a bit jaded."

"You need to get out and do some Christmassy things around the city to restore your love of the holidays." Olivia snapped her fingers. "You could go for hot chocolate at the winter village in Bryant Park and do some ice skating."

I arched an eyebrow at her. "By myself?"

"You could imagine that you're skating over your ex-boyfriend's face."

I laughed at this, even though the thought of Ethan and discovering his wandering ways after we'd been together for two years still made my gut twist. "That would make it more fun, but I don't think a family-friendly ice rink wants me hurling insults at my feet as I skate."

Olivia grinned. "I guess not, but you're not still that upset at him, are you?"

"Upset that I wasted two years of my life with a guy who probably never had any intention of settling down, at least, not with me? Upset that I found out he'd been cheating on me for half the time we were together? Upset that he broke up with me two days before my birthday so he wouldn't have to buy me a gift or take me to dinner?"

Olivia held up one palm. "Okay, that was particularly douchy, but you're better off without him. He was never going to step up and be the one. Catching him screwing around was the best thing that ever happened to you."

I wasn't sure if I'd classify walking in on my ex and his nubile Pilates instructor neighbor as the best thing that had ever happened to me, but I released a breath. "I guess you're right, but here I am, single and barreling toward Christmas and turning thirty alone."

"You don't turn thirty until next spring."

"It feels like it's right around the corner!"

Olivia reached over and put a hand on my knee. "Listen, you're beautiful, smart, funny, and you have an amazing work wife."

I couldn't suppress a laugh as I shook my head. "You are pretty amazing."

She winked at me. "I know, and so are you. You're going to find someone who sees all the things in you that I do."

I put my hand over hers. "Right back at you."

Olivia flipped her hand around to hold mine and gave it a squeeze. "Speaking of me finding my perfect guy…"

My warm feeling started to fade. "Please don't tell me you have another Tinder date."

"I have another Tinder date," she squealed.

"Liv, how many of these have you been on?"

"This month or this week?" She giggled. "It's only until I get selected to be a tribute bride for the Drexians."

"Even worse."

"How can being mated to a perfect, gorgeous, alien badass be worse?"

I knew that the planet had gone mad for the aliens who defended us, but the idea of going to live in space did not appeal, even if the aliens were hunky.

I shook my head. "These dates are always a disaster. I hate to see you waste your time."

"They're not a waste of time. I meet someone new, get a few drinks out of it—sometimes dinner or brunch—and usually a

9

great story to tell you later." She gave me a pointed look as she stood. "At least I'm getting out there."

Touché. Olivia was right that I hadn't started dating again, but hearing about her horrendous dates wasn't helping.

"What if it's another guy who knits hats for his cat—out of its own fur?"

My friend made a face. "What are the chances of there being two guys like that?"

"It's New York City. I'd say it's relatively high."

She waved a hand at me. "This guy won't be like that. He doesn't have cats. Only a Yorkie."

I wrinkled my nose. "He's a small dog guy?"

"Small dog guys can be hot. At least I know he's not overcompensating for something with a Great Dane."

Olivia retrieved her purse from under the desk, and I peeked at the tiny clock we kept tucked away from sight at the back of the desk. We still had an hour until the store closed and we could go home.

"Where are you going?" I stood quickly. "Is this date now?"

"No, but I'm meeting him for drinks right after work, and you know how crazy traffic is if I wait until the end of the day. I'll have to sit forever in an Uber or fight a million people on the subway."

I glanced at the appointment book open on the desk and jabbed my finger at the last name on the day's roster. "But you still have one more client."

She gave me a pleading look and put her hands together as if in prayer. "I know, but is there any way you could cover for me?"

I huffed out a tortured breath. "Do you really want to inflict my dour mood on an unsuspecting Upper East Side matron?"

"It's not a woman from the Upper East."

I squinted at the scrawl of her illegible handwriting. "A husband looking for gifts for his wife and mistress?"

She shook her head. "I promise this one will be interesting. We'll both have stories to tell tomorrow."

"Mine will be how I convinced a shopper to skip Christmas altogether and join the Peace Corps," I mumbled as my friend back away.

"You're the best."

"You owe me big," I called after Olivia, as she started bouncing on the balls of her feet in excitement. "Huge. Bigger than a blimp in the Macy's Thanksgiving Day parade."

I swept my gaze around after invoking the name of our competitor, but there was still no one near us.

"I love you." She blew me kisses as she turned on her heel and dashed from the Fifth Avenue Club.

"Love you too," I grumbled, as I sank back down in my chair. Despite my mood, I did admire how brave Liv was to keep dating, even if it did sometimes involve cat-fur hats. Maybe she was right. Maybe it was time for me to get back out there.

"After Christmas," I told myself as I searched for my shoes under the desk with my feet. There was no way I could handle dating and crazy holiday shoppers at the same time.

I groaned. Where had my heels gone? Dipping my head under the desk, I spotted my shoes and stretched out an arm to grab them.

"Hello?"

The voice was so deep that I jumped, banging my head on the underside of the desk. I quickly emerged, jamming my shoes on my feet as I tried to stand. I only had one on when I saw who was standing on the other side of the desk.

He was well over six feet tall—maybe close to seven—and it was clear he was all muscle and lots of it. But it wasn't his impressive physique underneath the form-fitting black uniform that made me drop my remaining shoe on the floor. It was his piercing blue eyes that matched his blue skin.

"Are you Olivia?"

CHAPTER 3

Griff

The quiet area of the busy store was a welcome change from the chaotic city, and I was even grateful that there were no humans in sight when I walked past the sign that read The Fifth Avenue Club in swirly alien letters.

I had done everything that the Drexian on the transport had instructed me to do. I had gotten into the long black car waiting for me at the landing pad and told the driver to take me to Saks Fifth Avenue in Manhattan. Dix had been very clear that it had to be the one in Manhattan, whatever that meant. I'd tried not to gape as we'd traversed the city, but the buildings that had been tiny as we'd approached in the ship now towered above me. They were not as high as the structures in the cloud city of Neboon, but they were solid and made of glittering steel.

Almost as surprising as the number of tall buildings were the lights. Every building seemed to be adorned with lights, and some had walls of glass with elaborate designs on display. I'd stood in front of the Saks Fifth Avenue store, staring at the colorful and changing lights that covered the entire massive building. It looked like an ice palace one moment and like it was wrapped in a giant red bow the next.

I'd finally stumbled inside and been directed to the personal shopping department, where I stood scanning the area that held little more than a dual level desk with tall windows behind it and an odd painting of black slashes on a stark, white background.

Rustling sounds behind the desk drew my attention. I was not alone. "Hello?"

There was a thunk under the desk, and a female with pale hair appeared. She stood quickly then performed an odd hop as she attempted to put a black shoe on her foot. Her bright smile faded when she saw me.

I ignored her surprise. Although I'd been assured that humans were familiar with the existence of creatures from other planets, I'd become very aware since stepping from my car and onto the sidewalk in front of the store that most of the aliens they had seen had been Drexians, who looked remarkably similar to humans, apart from their increased stature and the raised bumps that ran down their spines and stayed mostly out of sight. This female was not the first who had stared openly at my blue skin.

"Are you Olivia?"

She blinked at me for a while before giving her head a shake. "No, I'm not."

My eagerness faded. Dix had assured me that Olivia would take care of everything. "I have an appointment with Olivia. I was told she would be here."

"I'm Caroline." She hobbled forward before her cheeks flushed pink, and she scooped up her dropped shoe and jammed it on her foot. "Olivia had to go out, and she asked me to help you."

"You are a personal shopper as well? You can find all the things on my list?"

She touched a hand to her hair and squared her shoulders. "I am, and I'm happy to help you find everything on your list."

"I suppose it is tolerable that I work with you and not Olivia."

Her smile faltered. "Thanks."

I sensed from her tone that her gratitude was not genuine. "I do not mean that as an insult."

"It certainly sounded like a compliment."

Her words were agreeable, but the tone still did not match and her expression told me that she was not pleased. "Apologies, human. This is my first trip to Earth, and the Drexian on my transport arranged for me to meet with Olivia. He assured me that she could help me."

Her shoulders relaxed. "No, I'm sorry. I'm sure it was confusing if you were told to meet one person and got a different one instead. I assure you that I'm just as qualified as Olivia, and I will do my best to get you everything on your list."

I gave her a small bow with my head. "You have my gratitude. My name is Griff."

"It's nice to meet you, Griff." She walked fully from behind the desk to reveal a black dress that hugged her curves and matched her shoes, but even with the spikes on her shoes that made her taller, the top of her head still only reached my chin. She held out her hand.

I eyed it for a moment before remembering in the research I'd done on humans that many of them liked to touch hands when they greeted each other. I placed my palm to the surface of hers, even though my large hand dwarfed her small one. "It is nice to meet you, Caroline."

She dropped her hand with a confused expression. "I know you're not Drexian. Where are you from?"

"I am Valorian from the planet Valoria which resides in the far corner of the galaxy. We are a peaceful species, and we have recently joined the Drexian alliance against the Kronock."

"Then that makes us allies."

"It does. We have long admired the Drexians and their arrangement with Earth."

She scrunched her lips to one side and her soft green eyes sharpened. "You mean the tribute bride program."

I instantly sensed her displeasure. "You do not approve of the Drexians selecting human brides."

She shrugged. "I guess I don't have a problem with it if women want to spend their lives in space."

"Now all females wish to leave this overpopulated, overheated planet and journey to space?"

She folded her arms over her chest. "Some of us still like this crowded, hot planet."

"I did not mean to insult your planet. It is very twinkly."

The corners of her mouth twitched. "Twinkly?"

"Yes, there are twinkling lights everywhere. The front of this building is covered in them."

She put a hand over her mouth as she giggled. "Those are Christmas lights. The city isn't always so twinkly."

It was hard to imagine what the place would look like without the illumination. "That is too bad."

She mumbled something about more fans of Christmas before unfolding her arms. "We should probably get started on your list. How many people are we shopping for today, Griff?"

"We are only shopping for one."

Her brows lifted. "Oh? Is this for your wife perhaps? Did she send you all the way to Earth to buy her something?"

"This is not for a wife. I have no mate."

Her smile slipped. "Oh, sorry."

"Do not be sorry. That is why I am here."

She tilted her head at me. "What is why you're here?"

"The Drexians have had such good luck procuring mates from Earth, I thought that I would follow their lead."

Her brow furrowed. "You're here to get a tribute bride, and you want to buy her presents?"

I frowned. It was not as easy to explain as I had hoped. I pulled my device from my pocket and clicked it on so that my list was displayed on the screen. "I am not here to get a tribute bride, but I am here to find a human mate." I held the device to her. "This is the list of qualities I would like in the mate you find for me."

Caroline's gaze went from me to the device then back to me. "I'm sorry, what?"

CHAPTER 4

Caroline

 e couldn't be serious, could he? I gave my head a small shake. Maybe I'd heard him wrong. "Did you say you have a list of what you want in a wife, and you want me to find her for you?"

The massive alien tilted his head at me, his penetrating gaze studying my face. "That is correct. That is your job, is it not?"

"To play matchmaker?" I put my hands on my hips and scowled at him. "No, it's not my job."

I'd had clients ask me to find crazy things for them before—an alpaca fur coat dyed pink, a vintage Barbie and an even more vintage Allan, a Mont Blanc pen studded with actual rubies—but picking out a person was going too far. I opened my mouth to tell the alien exactly what I thought of him when a thought hit me.

Olivia.

This was her doing. I swiveled my body to take in the entire area, peering into the store to see if she was hiding within one of the racks of clothes. My friend was obviously punking me to try to cheer me up. Not that sending an alien to mess with me was the way to make me feel better about Christmas. "Where is she?"

Griff followed my gaze, twisting his body until he'd made a full rotation. "Where is who? The mate I would like you to find me? I do not know because—"

"Not that." I flapped a hand at him. "Where's Olivia? She put you up to this, didn't she?"

His blue brow wrinkled as he tipped his head to peer at the ceiling. "Put me up where?"

I ignored him, although I had to give him credit. He was very convincing. I took a few strides forward, my heels rapping on the tile. "O—li—via!"

If I'd expected her to appear after I'd sung her name, clutching her side with laughter at pulling a prank on me, I was disappointed. A few nearby customers glanced my way, but none of them were Olivia, and no one was holding a phone up to record.

"I am confused. Is Olivia here? You told me she wasn't."

I swiveled back to face Griff. "She wasn't, but she must be somewhere near watching this, right?"

"Why would she be watching this?"

I scrutinized Griff. If he was in on the gag, he was really going full Method. Then something else struck me, and my stomach sank. "Olivia didn't send you?"

"No, a Drexian named Dix sent me and told me to ask for Olivia." The alien's voice was steady, but I could sense that he was as confused as I was. "I have never met her."

19

I raked a hand through my hair as I walked blindly back to stand behind my desk. "This isn't a joke?"

"Why would I joke about such an important matter?"

I put my palms on the cool surface of the desk and leaned forward. "I don't know. Why would you come to a personal shopper to find a wife?"

The alien met my gaze with a sincere one of his own. "I do not understand human females, but you do. That is why you will be better at finding the perfect one for me."

I bit back a laugh, and it came out as a muffled snort. "Debatable."

"You do not understand human females?"

I released a breath. "Women are pretty different. I don't know if anyone could claim to understand every one of them. I think there are still some matchmakers out there, but honestly, I think half of that is for reality TV, and even the professionals aren't always successful."

The alien's gaze dropped to the floor. "Then I will have to return home empty-handed."

"I'm sure that won't be necessary."

I jerked at the shrill voice emerging from the nearby staircase leading to offices below. *Fuck, fuck, fuck.*

Of course, my boss had overhead *that.*

I straightened as Miranda's heels slapped the last few steps, a cloud of expensive perfume preceding her as she strode toward Griff with a solicitous smile on her face. Her dark hair was scraped into a tight bun, and her lipstick was such a bright shade of fuchsia it seemed to arrive before she did. "Clients of The Fifth Avenue Club do not go home empty-handed." Then she snapped her head to me, her expression hard. "What seems to be the problem, Caroline?"

"Nothing, Miranda." I forced myself to meet the woman's hard gaze. "We might not be the right choice for this gentleman's needs."

"Nonsense." Miranda released a high laugh, pivoting away from me and facing him. "We are honored that you chose the flagship Saks Fifth Avenue store for your shopping needs." She shot me a pointed look. "I'm sure Caroline will do everything in her power to find exactly what you need, won't you?"

It didn't take a genius to know that there was a threat implied in her look. Miranda was always subtly threatening to find salesclerks to replace us, especially if we asked for time off or a long lunch. She even gave us side eye for taking our allotted breaks. She'd made it clear many times over that our jobs were coveted and there was a long list of women eager to fill them.

I returned her fake smile. "Absolutely."

"Good." She nodded, as if pleased with herself and her ability to swoop in and solve problems. "Now I need to leave for an appointment." She put a hand on Griff's arm as she passed, her eyes flaring briefly with interest. "Thank you again for choosing Saks Fifth Avenue."

I fought the urge to roll my eyes as my supervisor left with a flirty wave to Griff. The woman had been alien-crazy since the Drexians had revealed themselves, and I was certain the only reason she hadn't applied to be a tribute bride was the age cutoff. More than once, Olivia and I had seen her scouring the gossip magazines for photos of the latest Drexian-human wedding, and it was clear from the way she'd eyed Griff that she had no issue with blue-skinned aliens.

A wicked part of me wanted to slap her hand in his and call it a day, but I wouldn't do that to the guy. Even if he was currently on my shit list and had gotten me in hot water with my bitchy boss.

Once Miranda had disappeared, I sighed and shook my head wearily. "I guess I don't have much of a choice."

The alien stared at me in obvious disbelief. "You will help me?"

"I honestly don't know how," I mumbled. "It's not like we stock single females in a range of sizes here, but I guess I'd better figure out something." I extended my arm and opened my palm. "Show me your list."

CHAPTER 5

Griff

I placed my device in Caroline's hand with my list displayed on the illuminated screen. I had created my requirements before I'd arrived on Earth and before I'd encountered my first human female, which might have been a mistake.

The female shopper glanced at the list and her eyes popped wide. She looked at me. "No mucus?"

I cleared my throat. "The females of Galleren Alpha exude a thin layer of mucus during the rainy season."

Her lips quirked up. "And you weren't a fan?"

I did not know why this would be amusing, if she was indeed on the verge of laughing. Obviously, she had never tried to clasp a mucus-covered hand in the rain. "I was not."

"Shouldn't be a problem. Humans don't exude."

"Good." I motioned to the device. "Should I amend the list?"

She handed it back to me, and I quickly removed that item from my list. I held it out to her again, but she waved me off.

"I won't need that."

I looked at the list I'd painstakingly drafted. "Why not?"

"That list doesn't have anything to do with what actually matters when it comes to finding a wife."

I glanced at my requirement that the female not spontaneously combust when exposed to static. That seemed like something that would matter if I wished to have a mate that survived visits to the lightning fields of Perria Prime.

"I don't know what kind of mates your people normally find, but you don't need to worry about mucus or excessive gills or poisonous tentacles with Earth women."

My face warmed. I had read a little about Earth but admittedly, I had been more interested in the planet's varied geography and violent history than in the types of females. "What about the tendency of humans to go to war? I would prefer a mate who does not incite uprisings."

Caroline grinned. "Now, where's the fun in that?"

I frowned, not sure if she was serious. Earth humor still confused me.

She sat down and patted the chair next to her. "If you want to make an actual list of qualities you want in a wife, I can help you do that."

As much as I did not want to waste the list I'd created, I supposed I should listen to the human's advice when it came to her own species. I sat, my knees brushing hers as our chairs faced.

She rolled her chair back a bit and pulled a pad of paper from a drawer. She picked up a silver pen from a cup filled with more metallic pens and tapped the end on the paper. "Usually, you start with any physical requirements like if you prefer someone tall or short or if you like any particular hair color." She held up a hand as I opened my mouth. "You don't need to worry about mucus or tentacles or gills."

I closed my mouth again. "I do not have any physical requirements aside from safety ones. I would prefer a female who isn't so large she would crush me. I also would like it if she wasn't so small that I could crush her."

Caroline held the pen over the paper. "I don't think that's much of a concern. You don't have a preference for blondes or brunettes?"

"What is a blonde?"

Color flushed her cheeks, and she curled a strand of her pale hair around one finger. "I'm a blonde. Not if I don't get my roots done soon, though." She laughed, but then dropped her gaze to the paper. "Blondes have light hair and brunettes have dark. Then there is black hair, red hair, gray hair—"

"Blue hair?"

"Yes, but not naturally."

"Females on my planet have blue hair, except for some who are born with pale-pink hair." I thought of my own mother's long, pink hair that had been almost translucent. "But all males have black hair."

Caroline's gaze went to my hair, which was cut short. "Tall, dark, and…" She darted her gaze back to the empty paper. "So, any hair color preference?"

I shook my head. "I do not have any preference regarding female appearance. I have seen beautiful creatures with all colors of skin, hair, and eyes since I have been here. Your green eyes are nice, even if they aren't blue."

"Gee, thanks." She didn't look up, and I sensed I had said something else wrong.

"It is just that Valorians have blue eyes, so I am accustomed…" My words faded as she shot me a look. "But I do not require blue eyes. I have no preference."

She gave a curt nod. "Good. That makes it easier."

I thought about the task I'd been given and the short amount of time allotted to it, although I didn't want to dwell on the reason. "I am more interested in compatibility."

Her stiff posture relaxed a bit. "Smart. So, common interests?"

"More like sexual compatibility. I need to know if my mate can handle the size of my—"

"Whoa, there!" Caroline held up her free hand, the pink of her cheeks now a much deeper hue. "That's not exactly something you can ask women."

"Then I will need to test them out."

"No!" She rolled her chair back. "You can't go around New York asking to test out women's…well, you can, but you're going to get weird looks. And the women who will agree to it probably won't be the kind of woman you'd want as a wife."

"No?"

She shook her head firmly. "That isn't the kind of thing you find out until you know someone a lot better." She dropped her voice. "Or have had a lot of drinks."

"Drinks help in finding a mate?"

She bobbled her head. "I mean, sometimes. A lot of couples do meet at bars."

"And these bars serve drinks? Enough drinks that would encourage a female to—?"

"Still, no." Caroline gave me a stern look. "I know you're a big guy, but you aren't bigger than the Drexians, and human women haven't had any issues with them."

I considered her reasoning. This was true. Drexian males were no smaller than Valorians, and they had been enthusiastic about their matings with human females. "You are correct."

She let out a breath. "So can we agree you aren't going to go around New York City trying to test out women?"

I slowly nodded. "I will agree to that."

"Good." She muttered something about saving me a night in jail, as she returned her gaze to the empty paper. "Now we should probably get something down on this new list."

"I would prefer a different strategy than the list."

She looked up. "You're abandoning the list?"

"I would like to put it on hold for now and try your other suggestion."

She narrowed her eyes. "My other suggestion? I don't remember making another suggestion."

I squared my shoulders and smiled at her. "I would like to go to one of these bars where couples meet."

She dropped her pen on the pad. "You're going to go to a bar?"

"*We* are going to go to a bar," I corrected. "You're going to take me."

CHAPTER 6

Caroline

"*T*his is such a bad idea," I said under my breath, as I led Griff out the front door of Saks Fifth Avenue.

"Wasn't there a bar inside the store?" Griff asked, glancing over his shoulder as we emerged into the sidewalk that was bustling with holiday shoppers and people heading home after work.

There was a bar inside Saks, but there was no way I was taking the alien to drink and potentially pick up women where I worked. I was already going against all my better instincts by taking the guy to a bar in the first place. Technically, I wasn't supposed to fraternize with customers outside work hours, but Miranda had made it clear that I needed to make Griff happy. Since the thing he wanted me to procure for him was a wife, the only way I was going to do that was by taking him from the store.

"This is your first time in New York, right?"

"That is correct."

I hooked my arm through his, more to keep from being separated in the crush of people pushing us than anything. "Then you should see more of New York."

I propelled us both away from Saks and around the corner. The December wind bit at my ankles, and I tugged my red coat with white polka dots tighter around my neck. It hadn't snowed yet, but the air carried the distinct scent of impending snow, which I knew would clog up the city.

Frigid weather was yet another thing I didn't love about the holiday season, and I ducked inside the wrought iron gates of a nearby courtyard and then through a set of glass doors. I stomped my feet to dispel some of the chill as I led Griff up sweeping staircases and past soaring columns until we were entering an ornate, gold room with a long bar and a high, domed ceiling.

He stared at the opulent surroundings as I tugged him behind me to two open stools at the bar. "I did not think Earth bars looked like this."

"Most of them don't," I admitted. I didn't tell him that it was one of the nearest bars to Saks and one I came to when I wanted to feel like I wasn't a struggling almost-30-year-old. The gilded-age glamor of the place always made me feel better, even during the madness of the holidays.

I didn't need to look at the drink menu to know what I wanted, but I pivoted to Griff in my stool. "What's your poison?"

His brows popped high, reminding me that universal translator implants didn't give context or explain popular sayings.

I laughed and shook my head. "It means what do you want to drink?" I leaned closer so he could hear me over the din of conversation. "I recommend the Hemingway or The Mrs. Astor."

He looked at me blankly. "I will take your recommendation."

I swiveled to face the bar, grabbing a bartender's attention and raising my voice. "Two Mrs. Astors."

Griff was already scanning the crowd, seemingly unaware of the stares he was attracting. Despite most people accepting the Drexians and the existence of aliens, not everyone was used to seeing the larger creatures walking among us. Blue-skinned aliens were definitely not the norm—yet.

"How does one meet females in such a crowd?" Griff asked as our cocktails were slid across the shiny bar toward us.

"First things first." I picked up my martini glass and lifted it. "Here's to finding you a wife."

Griff picked up his own glass and matched my movement, but he seemed perplexed.

I clinked my glass lightly to his. "Cheers!"

"Is this part of the human mating ritual?"

I almost spluttered the sip I was taking. "Not between us, obviously, but I guess so."

"Couples share cocktails in order to get to know each other better and loosen their inhibitions?"

"You could put it like that." I swallowed the sweet drink, glad that there was plenty of booze in it, even though the strawberry and lemon masked the taste.

Griff downed his cocktail in a single gulp and replaced the martini glass on the bar. "I have had a cocktail. Now what?"

I eyed the empty glass and then him. "I guess you nailed the drinking part. Now you need to look around and see if there are any women who appeal to you." I make a point of scanning the crowd at the bar. "Is there anyone you think looks interesting? Is there anyone who's making eye contact with you?"

"Aside from you?"

I took another sip and tried to ignore the flutter of my pulse. "Aside from me."

"There is one female who looks very interested."

I craned my head to follow his gaze. "That's good." I couldn't see through the crowd to the woman he meant, but he was considerably taller than me. "Do you want to go talk to her?"

"I do not need to go to her. She appears to be coming toward me."

I guess women weren't going to be shy here, especially if they had a thing for aliens. I hadn't had a chance to warn Griff about alien chasers, but now seemed like an awkward time to do it.

It isn't your job to vet women for him, Caroline. Just find him someone decent and call it a day.

Before I could gracefully turn away and give him some privacy, the woman burst through the crowd around us.

"Caroline?"

I gaped at my friend as she slid her gaze back and forth between me and Griff. "Liv?"

"Who's your friend?" she finally asked.

"This is the appointment you left me to cover." I tossed back the rest of my cocktail. "Griff, this is Olivia."

My friend's dark eyebrows shot so high they disappeared beneath her bangs. "Shut the front door."

I ignored her slack-jawed expression. "What happened to your date?"

"Disaster." She shook her head as she waved at the bartender. "Hit me with a martini and make it so dirty I blush."

Griff got off his barstool and motioned for Liv to take it. She gratefully hopped up, leaning over and whispering to me, "Please tell me you're not dating the clients."

"I'm not. This is the only way to get him what's on his list."

She flicked a gaze to Griff. "What's on the big guy's list?"

"A wife."

The bartender slid a martini toward Liv, and she tapped the rim of my empty glass and her full one. "You're going to need to keep these coming."

CHAPTER 7

Griff

*C*aroline's dark-haired friend, the Olivia I had originally been told to meet, eyed me over the top of her glass as she sipped the clear liquid. When she put the glass on the shiny bar and plucked out the tiny sword jammed with green-colored orbs, she pointed it at me. "Who told you to ask for me?"

"The Drexian on the transport that brought me here." I watched her bite one green ball from the mini sword. "Dix."

"A Drexian?" She tapped the tip of the small sword on her chin. "I wonder if it was the one who interviewed me."

"What does it matter?" Caroline nudged Olivia.

"I want to know who to have a word with, that's all. The Drexians should know that we don't sell wives at Saks Fifth Avenue."

I shifted from one foot to another and stepped closer to the women sitting on their barstools as I was jostled from behind by the growing crowd. "I might not have mentioned what was on my shopping list."

"That explains it." Olivia popped the final green ball into her mouth.

"It doesn't change anything." Caroline picked up the fresh drink the bartender slid her. "I still need to make the client happy." She took a generous swig. "Miranda's words, not mine."

Her friend sucked in a breath. "Miranda knows about him?"

Caroline nodded. "She caught me trying to explain that we don't procure mates at the personal shopping department, and basically told me to get him what was on his list, or she'd find someone who would."

"Talk about a Scrooge."

Caroline held up a finger. "An alien-obsessed Scrooge."

Olivia gave her friend a sideways glance. "So, Miranda threatened to fire you if you didn't find this guy a wife and you brought him here?"

Caroline downed the rest of her pale-pink drink. "Well, I wasn't going to find anyone in the shoe department."

"Good point." Olivia twisted her lips to one side. "Unless he's open to cute guys." She turned her attention to me. "Are you open to considering men?"

I thought about it for a moment before shaking my head. Unless human procreation worked differently than I'd heard, that would not work. "I would prefer a female."

"Too bad. Trevor is a catch."

Caroline exhaled loudly "Olivia, this isn't helping."

"Sorry." The dark-haired female swung her head from side to side. "I don't think this place will do you much good. It's a bit of a swordfight in here tonight."

"It was close, and it's freezing outside," Caroline said. "You know I hate the cold."

"Swordfight?" I cut my gaze to the tiny sword the female had discarded on a square napkin. If these were the swords being given out, it would not be much of a fight.

"You know, sausage fest, brodeo?"

I stared at the human who was making no sense. None of those phrases meant anything, according to my universal translator implant.

Caroline put a hand on my arm and leaned forward. "She means there are too many males and not enough females."

"Why didn't she just say that?" I said in a low voice to myself, wondering if coming to Earth had been a horrible mistake. I did not understand the culture, brides were not as easy to come by as the Drexians had made it seem, and even the language was confusing.

I looked at Caroline's hand that was still resting on my sleeve. Her fingers were long and slender with nails painted a light shade of pink, and they were drumming rhythmically on my arm. The movement didn't bother me, and I had a feeling she wasn't even aware she was doing it. It was actually somewhat comforting, and the soft heat of her palm through the fabric of my shirt reminded me that it had been a very long time since I'd enjoyed a female's touch.

"Um, Caroline."

Olivia's voice startled both Caroline and me. She darted her gaze to her hand on my arm, glanced up at me watching her, and then jerked her hand away.

"My bad." She gave me a quick, apologetic smile. "The fabric of your shirt is nice."

Olivia sighed. "Before we go down a weird textile rabbit hole, I have an idea."

More phrases that made no sense. I saw no small creatures with large ears and could not imagine one of their holes anywhere in the crowded bar.

Olivia held up a device. "We don't need to go bar hopping when we have this."

Caroline groaned. "We are not going to find Griff a wife on Tinder."

I squinted at the screen and the round images of human males lined up down the left side. "What is Tinder?"

"Not where you find a wife," Caroline said.

"You just hate Tinder because you met what's-his-name on Tinder." Olivia flipped her phone around. "We don't have to use Tinder. There's Bumble. There's also Bristlr, but that's just if you're interested in guys with beards, and we've already established that you're hetero. Match is a little old-school, but if you're looking for wifey material, that might be our best bet."

"Is she still speaking an Earth language?" I asked Caroline.

"Kind of. She's talking about using dating apps." When I didn't reply, she added. "Algorithms to match you with potential mates."

That did not sound so bad. The Drexians used an algorithm now to match their warriors with human mates.

"Smile!" Olivia held her device in front of my face.

I was too startled to smile, but she clicked a button and lowered the device anyway.

"That's good. You look tough. Women will like that."

"What are you doing?" Caroline craned her neck to peer over her friend's shoulder, but Olivia angled her body away.

Olivia made a few final taps and grinned. "Setting up his profile." She flipped her screen around to show an image of my face along with my name underneath.

Caroline scrutinized it for a beat before snatching the device. "Likes hot cocoa and ice skating? Enjoys long walks through the park?"

Olivia shrugged. "It's vague and harmless. Who doesn't like those things?"

"Maybe someone who isn't from Earth?"

"If you really need to find this guy a wife, we should give this a try." Olivia took back her phone, her eyes widening. "He's already getting matches."

Caroline's fingers drummed on her own leg as she frowned at her friend, and I got the feeling that she wasn't pleased, which made even less sense than an algorithm finding me a mate.

CHAPTER 8

Caroline

hy did I care if Olivia had walked in and taken over me finding a wife for Griff? It wasn't like I wanted to be stuck with the alien's bizarre request. It was supposed to have been her appointment, anyway.

An appointment she'd begged me to take so she could leave early for her date. I'd agreed, which meant that by our established rules of selling, she'd forfeited all rights to work with him or make commissions. In this case, there wouldn't be commissions, but it was the same thing, wasn't it?

I shook my head, trying to shake off the muddled feeling that was no doubt thanks to the multiple Mrs. Astor cocktails. I should be happy that Olivia was here giving me a hand. I didn't want to be working overtime to finish this client's list, even if Griff was the most intriguing customer I'd had all week.

I snuck a glance at him as Olivia eagerly showed him the women matching with him on her phone. Sure, he was tall, which I liked in a guy, and big without being hefty. His square jaw and dark hair made classically handsome, even though his blue skin was anything but typical. While it had been startling at first, I barely noticed it now. What I did notice was that he had a nice smile, when he smiled, which wasn't often.

Not that I was an alien chaser. I wasn't. Far from it. I'd been as curious as anyone when the Drexians had revealed themselves, but I rolled my eyes at the women who'd lined up to volunteer as tribute brides. Human men might not be as exciting as alien warriors, but I was fine keeping my feet firmly planted on Earth, thank you very much.

"What was that?" Olivia looked over her phone at me.

Crap. Had I said any of that out loud? It was still buzzing with loud enough conversations that I doubted she could have heard much, but the drinks were definitely stronger than I'd thought. It didn't help that I'd worked through lunch, which meant the booze had gone straight to my head.

"Nothing." I slid off my barstool, landing on my heels without falling over, which was a true Christmas miracle. "Since you've got this in hand, I'm going to head home."

"You sure?" Olivia didn't look as tipsy as I felt, and I wondered if she'd managed to get some food on her disaster of a date.

"Positive." I patted Griff's arm. "I know he's in good hands."

The alien narrowed his eyes at me. "You are walking to your home alone?"

I pulled my own phone from my purse. "I'll call a Lyft." When his brow wrinkled in confusion, I added. "It means a car will come pick me up."

He frowned at this, making him look very fierce. "I will escort you to this vehicle."

I fluttered a hand at him but used my other to grip his arm tighter so I wouldn't topple to the floor. "You don't have to do that. I'm a big girl."

He put a hand on my back. "You are hardly big at all."

"Let him walk you out," Olivia said, tapping wildly at her phone. "I'm already adding *chivalrous* and *protective* to his profile."

The crowd parted for us as Griff led the way toward the exit, one hand extended in front of us and one still on the small of my back. I tried to ignore the warm tingles that were spreading through my body, which were definitely from the drinks and not from his touch.

Once we left the bar, I realized just how loud it had been inside. My ears rang, and the sound of my shoes tapping the hard stone floor echoed as we made our way through the ornate building and outside.

I gasped as we stepped through the glass doors and onto the sidewalk. "I think it's gotten colder."

"Is all of your planet this cold?" Griff did not look cold, despite him literally being blue. He wasn't shivering like me or rubbing his hands briskly up and down his arms to stay warm.

"Nope. I hear the Caribbean is nice and toasty right about now." I peered up at the dark sky, surprised that snowflakes weren't drifting down already. "But they don't get to have the possibility of a white Christmas like we do."

"What is a white Christmas?"

"When we get enough snow to cover the ground on Christmas Day, it's called a white Christmas." I lowered my voice conspiratorially. "Don't tell Liv, but even I think white Christmases are nice."

He nodded solemnly. "I will keep your secret."

This made me giggle as I walked carefully toward the street with Griff at my side. If I stood close enough to him, his body blocked the wind. Besides, for a blue guy, he gave off a decent amount of body heat. Not to mention the fact that he smelled nice, like fresh laundry with a hint of something spicy. I wondered if it was a natural Valorian scent or if he was wearing some kind of alien cologne.

"You are not what I expected," I said once we were standing on the curb with a steady stream of traffic passing by us. I glanced at my phone and registered that my ride was a minute away.

"What did you expect?"

"From an alien who came to Earth searching for a mate?" I bobbed my head back and forth. "I guess I would have thought you'd be bossier about what you wanted."

"Bossy?"

"Yeah," I said, making my voice gruff. "'Bring me a buxom female to bear me babies.'"

A sound came from his throat that was almost like a laugh. "That is not what I sound like or what I would say."

"I know." I put a hand over my mouth to stifle another giggle. "That's what I mean. You want a wife, but you can't tell me what you like in women." I blew out a breath that was visible in the frigid air. "I guess it's nice to know that even a big, tough alien doesn't know what he wants either."

A dented, gray Toyota pulled up and the driver leaned across the passenger's seat. "Caroline?"

I really needed to start using Lyft preferred.

"That's me." I turned to Griff, who was eyeing the car with unguarded suspicion. "Good luck with Olivia and the dating apps."

He didn't speak as I patted his chest. I considered giving him a peck on the cheek, but I knew that was the Mrs. Astor cocktails making more bad suggestions. Instead, I spun around and got in the back seat of the car. Before I could close the door, Griff was getting in beside me.

"What are you doing?" I asked as I scooted across the backseat to accommodate his bulk.

"The females in the device can wait until I make sure you are home safely." He slammed the door shut, making the driver wince and curse under his breath. "You may proceed, Mr. Lyft."

The driver tapped the GPS on his mounted phone screen and shook his head. "Why do I get all the crazies?"

CHAPTER 9

Griff

"I swear, you don't need to do this." Caroline's voice was slurred as she stepped from the vehicle, taking my hand as I helped her over a puddle of murky water and onto the sidewalk. "I can get home by myself. I do it all the time."

I gave the shabby car that had smelled slightly of feet another scowl. "In a vehicle like this?"

"Maybe they aren't all like this." She closed the car door, and the driver took off, leaving her with her mouth open. "I guess we would have had to call you another ride anyway, but that was a bit rude, wasn't it?"

I did not understand Earth customs enough to say what was rude or not, but I was relieved that I was no longer crammed uncomfortably in the backseat of a smelly vehicle.

Caroline let go of my hand and started to dig around in her bag. "Now, where are my keys?"

The street we were now standing on was nothing like the busy one we'd left. Instead of towering, steel buildings reaching into the sky and the air being filled with blaring horns and sirens, the area was quieter and the buildings lower. There were more vehicles parked on both sides of the street than moving down it, and the buildings were constructed of matte stone instead of metal.

"Seriously, where are my keys?" Now Caroline was madly pawing in her purse, and she finally squatted and placed it on the sidewalk so she could use both hands.

"You require keys to get into your apartment?"

She peered at me for a beat before huffing out an exasperated breath. "Yes, and they aren't here." She waved one hand at the stairs leading up to a tall wooden door. "My neighbor usually has a spare, but I needed it last week and forgot to give it back to her."

I assessed the door. "Would you like me to remove it or break it down?"

"What? No!" She swiped a strand of hair from her face. "That would definitely not be a good look, especially since I'm subleasing."

She trudged to the bottom step and sank onto it, letting her purse sit between her feet. "I must have dropped my keys when I was cleaning out my purse at work. That's the only explanation."

"Should we return to the store?"

Caroline shook her head. "It's closed. There's no getting in until tomorrow morning." She jerked a thumb behind her at the door at the top of the stairs. "And there's no getting in there without keys. I would call Olivia, but she has about a dozen roommates, each one more judgy than the last. I'd rather sleep on my stoop than go there."

I could not imagine that Earth was so primitive that it used physical keys to secure dwellings, or so many people sharing a space, but so far, the planet had not been what I had expected. Neither had my personal shopper.

I stared at the female whose head hung between her slumped shoulders, her pale hair falling over the shoulders of her red coat. So far, she had not found any eligible mates for me to choose, although from what I understood, finding mates was not what her job typically entailed. I'd imagined that I would come to the human world, provide my list of requirements, and select from an offered assortment of females. Instead, I'd gone to a crowded bar that Caroline had deemed a sausage celebration and been loaded into a device that would provide matches for me. That device, I remembered, was back at the bar with Caroline's friend.

For some reason, I had no desire to return to review my matches with Olivia. Even if there were absolutely no females in sight, I preferred to stay with Caroline.

Odd, I thought. I usually preferred to spend my free time with other Valorian warriors. Despite our initial difficulty in understanding each other, I had enjoyed my close proximity to the pale-haired human. Her touch made my pulse increase and my chest tighten, but that would probably happen with any human female.

Then I thought about why I was on Earth, and my chest tightened in an uncomfortable way and without warmth spreading across it like it did when Caroline touched me. I should not waste time with a female who was not considering me as a mate—not when I had so little time on the planet—but I didn't want to dwell on my urgency to find a bride. Not now.

I held out my hand, and Caroline looked at me blankly.

"I am giving you a second chance."

She tilted her head and pursed her lips. "A second chance at what? This day? Yes, please."

"No." I took her by the hand and pulled her to her feet. "I have decided to give you a second chance to find me a mate."

She groaned. "Are we still doing this?"

"Since I am very far from your friend and her device matching system, I would like to give you a second chance to find me the perfect mate."

Caroline looked around the darkened street. "Now?"

"No. You need to sleep."

"No kidding," she mumbled. "Mrs. Astor was not my friend tonight."

"Can you get Mr. Lyft to return for us?"

She blinked at me as she retrieved her phone. "Where are we going?"

"You are coming back to my hotel with me." When her mouth opened to protest, I added quickly, "To sleep. Tomorrow, you will resume working on my list."

She cast a forlorn look at her building before shaking her head. "I guess I don't have much of a choice, but there are so many things wrong with this." She paused with her finger hovering over her screen. "Please tell me you aren't staying in some kind of alien hostel I don't know about."

I remembered the name of the hotel that had been arranged for me. "I do not believe it is a hostel, although I do not know what that is. I was told it was a plaza."

CHAPTER 10

Caroline

"*T*he Plaza?" I couldn't stop gaping as we walked through the revolving door of the hotel. "You're staying at *The* Plaza?"

My heels were muffled by the Persian carpet on the floor as I tipped my head up to take in the illuminated crystal chandelier and gilded cream ceiling. A Christmas tree towered in front of us, glittering white lights and gossamer cream ribbons adorning every branch. Glimmering gold boxes surrounded its base. Enormous mirrors covered the wall directly in front of us and behind the tree, which was flanked by two equally tall, narrow mirrors. I breathed in the scent of the fresh pine as we proceeded through the high doorway to the left and into another breathtaking room with more twinkling chandeliers.

My feet tapped the white marble floor as we proceeded past a bar tucked in a corner and a collection of small tables surrounded by arched-back upholstered chairs. Soaring windows lined the walls, and I imagined that the room was bright and sunny during the day. Since it was dark outside, the classical piano music leant the space an elegant, almost intimate feel.

Griff led the way past bannisters and columns wrapped in green garland to the long, dark wood reception desk that was also topped with lush arrangements of red flowers. "I believe there is a room for me reserved by the Drexian High Command."

A woman in a navy suit and crisp, white blouse didn't even ask his name. She tapped briskly on her keyboard, finally smiling up at us and sliding a paper folder containing key cards across the gleaming surface. "I hope you enjoy your stay at the Plaza."

"Thank you." Griff took the cream paper folder and turned to the elevator bank across from the desk.

"The Drexian High Command?" I whispered as I walked quickly beside him. "The Drexian big-wigs are putting you up at The Plaza?"

One of the elevator cars stood open, and we stepped inside. Luckily, we were alone.

"I do not think any Drexians wear wigs," Griff said.

I ignored this as the gold elevator doors closed and we surged up. "Who are you, really?"

"I have told you. My name is Griff, I am Valorian, and I am on Earth to find a mate."

I eyed him with suspicion. It might be all the cocktails lowering my inhibitions and eliminating my usual hesitancy to call someone's bluff, but I shook my head. "I don't believe that's your whole story. It can't be. As far as I know, the Drexians have never sent a Valorian here bride hunting before."

He swiveled his head to me. "Were you aware of the Drexians' activities before they revealed them to you?"

I opened and closed my mouth. He had a point. The Drexians had been taking Earth women for decades before they had revealed it publicly, and no one had been the wiser except the government officials who knew about the contract signed between the aliens and Earth. It was possible that Griff wasn't the first Valorian to come to Earth. Then I studied his blue skin. It was possible, but not very probable.

The elevator dinged softly as we reached our floor, and the door slid open. Griff extended his arm so that I could exit first; I stepped out and waited for him.

"You're telling me that you're no one special?" I followed him down the carpeted hallway, as he studied the ornate numbers on the doors. "I might not be one of the alien chasers who's submitted her name to be matched with a Drexian, but I know how it works. Even with all the women eager to land a Drexian, there's a hierarchy about which warriors get brides first."

Griff stopped in front of a door and held his hand to the locking mechanism. When nothing happened, he leaned in and held one eye in front of the peephole. Then he frowned and cleared his throat. "Open."

I pressed my lips together to keep from laughing. "The Plaza might be fancy, but it's not biometric-technology or voice-activation fancy." I took the paper folder from his hand, took out the key card and pressed it to the lock. When the door made a sound and the lock flashed green, I pushed down the knob and opened the door. "Voilà."

"Voilà?" He said to himself as he followed me inside.

Again, my mouth fell open as I walked through the suite. As opulent and classic as the rest of the hotel, the sitting room held a vignette of beige, tufted chairs and a love seat, with more fresh flowers in a bowl on the low, glass coffee table. I stepped from my heels, grateful to finally be able to free my feet, and padded to the doorway that led to the attached bedroom.

Not surprisingly, the bed was covered in pristine, white linens and a profusion of white and dove-gray pillows. A swath of matching gray fabric was swagged from high above to create a headboard, and lamps on the matching wooden night tables let off a warm glow.

"Are you tired?" Griff walked past me into the bedroom and sat on the pale-blue velvet chair in front of the nearby writing desk.

I was suddenly struck by the fact that there was one bed and two of us. As the effects of the potent cocktails began to fade, I realized that I was alone in a hotel room with a massive alien who was much stronger than me. And he had come to Earth with mating on the mind.

Not your smartest move, Caroline.

I backed from the room. "Actually, I'm not tired at all. I'm starving."

CHAPTER 11

Griff

"This is a club sandwich?" I eyed the stack of items held together by a decorated sliver of wood.

Caroline hungrily eyed the pair of plates the room service waiter had arranged on the coffee table in the sitting room as she sat on the couch for two. She snagged a long, yellow straw from her plate. "And fries. The perfect late-night food."

"Isn't a club a blunt weapon used in primitive societies? This does not look like one of those." I stood across from her and picked up one of my own fries and dropped it quickly, startled by how hot it was.

"Be careful. It seems like they just came out of the fryer." Caroline took another bite of hers. "Good question about the club sandwich. I have no idea why it's named that."

I had not done much research on human food because I'd been assured that it was bland and nothing to worry about. Not like the food on Kerlon One, which was eaten while in flames, or the cuisine on Zabloria, which was poisonous to any species but theirs.

"You should eat before the fries get cold." She'd discarded her red coat over the back of a chair and now slid to one end of the long seat as she tugged her black dress lower on her thighs. "Cold fries aren't great."

I hesitated before sitting. Since I'd entered the bedroom, the female had been jumpy. She claimed to be hungry, but she hadn't met my eyes since she'd placed the order over the rudimentary communication device, and she hadn't made a move toward that room again.

I finally sat down next to her while being careful not to let my legs touch hers, even though the creamy skin on her legs beckoned me to touch it. "What happens to cold fries? Are they toxic?"

She paused a fry that was halfway to her mouth. "You really don't know much about Earth, do you?"

"I do not." I picked up another fry, this time more gingerly, and took a bite at the end. Salty and both crunchy and soft on the inside. Not altogether unpleasant.

"So, why do you want a human wife?"

"The Drexians speak highly of your kind."

She laughed. "That can't be the only reason. You don't even know much about us." She waved a fry at me. "You thought we exuded slime."

"I am glad you do not."

"Same." Caroline took the decorative stick from her sandwich and picked it up. "I know that Olivia kind of took over finding you a match, but you should definitely learn more about us and what you like and don't like before you end up with someone you can't stand."

I watched her take a bite of the colorful stacked concoction. "There are human females you think I would dislike?"

She almost choked on her mouthful, holding up a finger as she swallowed. "Of course. Aren't there Valorians you dislike?"

I thought about the many Valorians I did not like. "There are."

"It's the same with human women. Some of us are delightful." She grinned. "But some of us put the itch in b—"

A sharp rap at the door cut her off, and I jumped at the sound. "Is there more food?"

"Not that I ordered."

I stood and crossed to the door, opening it cautiously. Another room service waiter stood in the hall with another rolling trolley. "We did not order additional food."

"This is a gift from the hotel manager to thank you for choosing The Plaza."

I backed up to allow him to wheel in the trolley and set the silver ice bucket on the table along with a pair of glasses.

Caroline's eyebrows popped high. "Champagne?"

"A gift from The Plaza," the waiter said again. "Would you like me to open it?"

"I'm not going to say no to Dom."

I was not sure if Caroline was calling the waiter Dom or the drink. The human language called English continued to baffle me.

The man deftly removed a metal cage from the top of the bottle, then removed the foil, covered the cork with a white cloth, and twisted the bottle until there was a surprising pop. He poured two glasses, which filled with bubbles, before replacing the bottle in the ice and giving a small bow as he backed from the room.

I lifted the bottle from the bucket filled with ice then glanced at the bubbling liquid. "This is a typical beverage?"

Caroline glanced at the matte-gold label that resembled a shield. "I wouldn't say typical. It's an expensive one. The hotel must be really excited to have you staying here."

Suspicion tinged her voice, but I did not tell her why the hotel might wish to impress me. I did not want her to know anything that might alter her opinion of me. I experienced enough of that on my home world. As far as Caroline knew, I was just another alien looking for a mate on Earth. I needed for her to believe that.

Caroline picked up one of the glasses and took a sip. "Who knew this would go so well with fries and club sandwiches?" She put down her glass. "Weren't we talking about you and your search for the perfect woman?"

I took a careful sip from my glass, but the bubbles were pleasant. "I do not require perfection."

"Good, because you won't find it."

I took another drink and let the bubbles tickle the back of my throat as I swallowed. "I would like a mate who is understanding."

Her eyes widened. "Finally. Now that's the kind of thing we can put on a list. What else?"

As I stared at her, I was hit by a pang of regret that Caroline did not want to take an alien mate. Despite all the missteps, my evening with her had been the best I had spent in a very long time.

She is tasked with finding your mate, I reminded myself. She cannot be yours, even if she'd expressed any desire for you, which she has not.

CHAPTER 12

Caroline

I leaned back and studied my decimated sandwich and fries. There were only bits of crust and a few untouched fries remaining on my plate. Even Griff's plate was clean, since the alien had warmed up to the fries and practically inhaled the sandwich.

My champagne flute was also empty, but I knew better than to drink any more. Luckily, the food had dampened my buzz, but I did not want a headache in the morning.

Thinking about the morning made my mind naturally turn to where I'd be waking up and where Griff would. I snuck a look at the broad-shouldered alien next to me, who was also leaning back and looking relaxed and sated.

I didn't know enough about the Valorians to know if I needed to be concerned about their sleeping habits or social expectations, but so far, Griff had been a perfect gentleman. He hadn't made a single move, which I tried not to take as an insult, since the guy had come to Earth looking for a wife and had also suggested test-driving potential mates, so to speak.

Not that you're looking for a husband, I reminded myself. It seemed like I had been one of the few single women in New York who hadn't swooned at the idea of a Drexian warrior. Not that it was the Drexians' fault. After my last disastrous relationship ended, I'd sworn that men in the city were all liars and cheats. So far, I hadn't lifted my dating embargo—not even for hot aliens.

My phone buzzed from inside my purse, and I jerked up. Olivia!

I snatched my bag from the floor and fumbled for the vibrating phone. I'd completely forgotten that we'd left Olivia at the bar waiting for Griff to return. "Crap, crap, crap, crap."

Griff straightened as he watched me, the placid mood shattered as I tapped my screen and saw the many unread texts from my friend.

U home?

Caroline?

Do u know where Griff is

He didn't come back to the bar

Hello?

"This is so bad," I muttered as I quickly typed a response. "*Sorry Liv. Phone was on mute. Griff went back to his hotel.*"

Three little dots flashed in the text bubble. *Too bad—his profile is blowing up.*

That didn't surprise me, considering how crazy for aliens the world had gotten since the Reveal. *Anyone good?*

Dunno. What's his type?

Great question. I doubted *understanding* was a quality that shined in online profiles. Before I could answer, the text bubble flashed again.

He's trending on socials.

That stopped me. How could he be trending on social media? He'd only been on the planet for a day, hadn't he?

I turned to Griff. "You didn't talk to anyone in the media, did you?"

He frowned. "The media?"

"Newspapers, TV, radio, podcasts?"

He crinkled his nose as if he'd inhaled something rancid. "I spoke to no one but you and your friend."

Another text from Olivia popped onto my screen. This time it was a link, which I clicked. Instantly, my screen was filled with images of Griff that were posted under the hashtag #bluealien. I shouldn't have been surprised that so many photos had been taken as we'd walked from Saks to the bar, while we were at the bar, and even outside the bar heading for my Lyft.

What made my stomach lurch were the number of photos featuring me next to Griff. When I scrolled down to one of Griff pulling me up from the steps in front of my building, my pulse leapt. The way the photo was taken, it looked like Griff and I were holding hands, and that I was staring up into his eyes. Butterflies danced in my throat as I remembered the moment and the warmth of his hands. Then I fought the urge to groan out loud.

Who had taken this? I would have sworn we were alone on the sidewalk, but I guess you were never alone in New York.

Someone was always watching, and with today's phones, always filming.

If my boss saw these, she would not be impressed. She'd fired personal shoppers for even the hint of impropriety with clients, and here I was holding hands with one. If she knew I was in his hotel room, I'd be out of a job before I could say "club sandwich."

This was not good. I couldn't let Olivia know what had happened or that I'd ended up back at The Plaza hotel with Griff. She was my friend, but this was hard to explain without me sounding like a hot mess. Besides, a part of me didn't want anyone knowing that I was with Griff because then it would seem sordid, which it wasn't.

I had a feeling that no one would believe I was his personal shopper searching for his future wife. Especially not since people were already posting comments on the photos asking who the "blondie" was and adding the hashtag #blondeandblue.

I swiped up to close the app, not wanting to read any more comments about me and Griff. Not that there was a "me and Griff," I reminded myself.

I read Olivia's final text—*Off to bed talk tmrw*—and dropped my phone back in my purse.

"You look unhappy."

I turned to Griff, so caught up in my own worries that I was almost surprised by his voice. "I'm not unhappy." I gave him an artificially bright smile. "It's just social media blowing everything out of proportion again."

"About me?"

"I guess lots of people spotted you around town today." I sighed. "You're trending."

"Is that a good thing or a bad thing?"

I held up a finger. "That's the million-dollar question, isn't it?" His eyes widened, and I couldn't help laughing. "Not literally a million dollars. I meant that it's a really good question, and a hard one to answer."

"Will this make it easier to find me a mate?"

Griff's gaze held mine so intently that my breath caught in my throat. I felt like telling him that it would help if he was interested in gold diggers or alien chasers, but I didn't want to frighten the guy. Besides, it was my job to find someone for him who wasn't like that. Suddenly, finding a mink bikini or a signed first edition of *Pride and Prejudice* didn't seem like much of a challenge by comparison.

He stood abruptly. "We are both tired. We should go to bed."

I thought about the one beautiful bed in the next room. "This is your suite. I'll take the couch."

He made a sound of derision in the back of his throat. "You will sleep in the bed."

His voice was so commanding, my jaw dropped, and heat arrowed through me. Was he ordering me to bed with him? I opened my mouth to offer a protest, even if it was going to be pathetic, since my voice seemed to have stopped working.

"I will sleep on the floor," he continued. "I am accustomed to hard bunks anyway."

Without waiting for my reply, he dropped to the floor on the other side of the coffee table, stretching his body across the carpet and folding his hands behind his head. Since his eyes were already closed and the matter appeared decided, I turned off the lamps in the sitting room, tiptoed into the bedroom, shed my work clothes, and slipped between the luxuriously soft sheets.

As my eyes fluttered shut, my thoughts drifted to the alien asleep on the hard floor so a virtual stranger in need could sleep in his bed, and I wondered how I was going to find someone good enough for Griff.

CHAPTER 13

Griff

*L*ight streamed across my face, and I draped an arm over my eyes to block it. I had been truthful that I was accustomed to sleeping in hard bunks, but what I was not used to was the bright sunlight on Earth. Since I'd spent a good deal of my life in space and on deep-space vessels, natural light was not common.

I dropped my arm and sat up, blinking at the rays pouring in through the sheer fabric covering the tall windows. Now that it was light outside, I could see that the room led onto a space with some greenery that could clearly withstand the cold weather.

The remnants of our meal from the night before were still on the coffee table, and the bottle bobbed in the bucket that was now filled with water instead of ice. Although the fries had seemed unusual at first, I would not have minded another plate full of them. Did humans also eat the hot, crunchy sticks in the morning?

I stood and brushed trace amounts of lint from my dark clothing that was wrinkled from being slept on. Additional clothing should be waiting for me somewhere in the suite, but I suspected it was in the bedroom where Caroline still slept. Thoughts of the human made my heartbeat quicken and thinking of her sleeping in my bed made heat skitter across my skin.

I needed to purge myself of these thoughts if I was to proceed with my task of finding a mate. I might not know all the things I wanted in a mate, but I knew that Caroline would have fulfilled all of them. If she had any interest in me, which it was clear she did not. She would not continue searching for a mate for me if she wished to be considered.

My pocket vibrated, reminding me that I had a device and that I had forgotten to check in and report my progress the day before. I walked to the glass doors leading to the outside, opening them and stepping into the crisp morning air before retrieving my communicator.

I pressed a finger to the screen to accept the transmission, and a familiar blue face filled the screen.

"I am glad to see you survived your first day on the alien world."

I bit back a sharp retort as I glanced at the wide-open space surrounded by more hotel rooms. "I did."

"And?"

I shifted from one foot to the other as I took in the frost-covered garden and empty fountains that stretched the entire length of the inner courtyard. "I have not found a mate yet, but I am looking."

"I was shown some images of you looking." He emphasized the last word, and I suspected he was not impressed by whatever images he'd seen. Maybe they were the same ones Caroline had been frowning at the night before. "You were with a female."

"I have engaged a personal shopper to assist in my search."

"You have hired help?" He nodded approvingly. "That is good. You should have the entire planet working for you."

"I do not need the entire planet to work for me," I said a bit too forcefully. "That is not how Earth operates."

A rough grunt indicated that he didn't approve of that. "As long as you return with a suitable bride."

"I will." The cold air felt good after the heat of the hotel, but I was eager to disengage and return inside. It was hard enough to complete my mission without being reminded that I had little time.

"From what I have been told, there are many females eager to meet you."

I thought back to Olivia using her device to find matches for me. "Earth has very different ways of finding mates, but I believe my shopper will find me the best one."

"The female with the light hair is your employee?"

I didn't like to think of Caroline as my employee since she technically did not work for me. I also did not want to explain the peculiar job of fulfilling wish lists. "She is."

"You are sure she is not one of the females you are considering?"

"She is not." This was partially a lie and partially the truth.

"Why not?"

The sharp question startled me into answering quickly. "I do not believe she is looking for a mate for herself."

A snort of derisive laughter. "Does she know who you are?"

"No." I glanced over my shoulder at the closed door. "No one on Earth does, and that is the way it will remain. I am doing this my way, remember?"

He huffed out an exasperated breath. "This could all be simplified, if the human females knew that you were the future emperor of Valoria."

That was exactly what I did not want them to know. I'd made great efforts to hide my identity when I'd served on space vessels, and I had not revealed my full name to any of the Drexians. My closest friends knew my lineage and my destiny, but they had learned it only after I had ascertained they were true friends. The last thing I wanted was a mate who desired me only for my position. "I should go."

"I do not need to remind you that you do not have much time left on Earth?"

When I had bargained for my journey to the human home world, I had been given three Earth days to find a mate. I had already used one. "You do not."

"Good." Then the screen flickered, and my father, the current emperor of Valoria, was gone.

I shoved the device back into my pocket. To say that my father had been reluctant to allow me to look for a mate on Earth would have been an understatement. If our own females had not been inexplicably dwindling and the Drexians hadn't been so successful repopulating their species with human mates, he never would have allowed it.

"There is much I will change when I rule Valoria," I whispered to myself, as I stepped back inside the hotel and was met by warm air and quiet. But first, I needed to prepare for another day looking for my future mate, and that required me to look like I hadn't slept on the floor and in my clothes.

CHAPTER 14

Caroline

$\mathscr{T}$he sound of rushing water tickled the back of my brain as I rolled over and stretched my arms. Was there a waterfall nearby? As I drifted from sleep to waking, I brushed aside the fantastical image of a waterfall. Maybe it was raining, although it didn't sound like the patter of rain. Then another thought hit me, had one of the pipes in my aging building broken again? That possibility made me sit bolt upright as I swung my head from side to side, half expecting to see water covering the floor.

But I wasn't in my apartment with the drafty windows and ancient pipes. I wasn't sleeping in my double bed under a tired, floral comforter. I ran my hands along the top of the pristine, white duvet and swept my gaze around the room. This was definitely not the West Village.

The night before came back to me in a rush. I was in The Plaza Hotel with the alien who'd booked me to find him a wife. We'd had club sandwiches and Dom Perignon, and then he'd slept on the floor in the sitting room and insisted I take the bed, which had been heavenly.

I was aware of the sound of water again, and I looked toward the bathroom door, which was slightly ajar. Unless I was mistaken, Griff was no longer asleep on the floor. He was in the shower. His dark clothes were draped over the marble counter near the door, and some deep-throated humming mingled with the sound of the water.

Steam drifted into the room along with the scent of expensive body wash, although I had a feeling it might be called something more elegant at The Plaza. Shower gel? Maybe they used a fancy French word for it. Whatever they called it, the aroma reminded me of being in a spa.

I couldn't help looking through the steam to the distinctive blue figure, although all I could see through the glass was a silhouette. An impressive silhouette that made my mouth go dry.

I jerked my head away, scolding myself for even trying to peek. "Look who's an alien chaser now."

My cheeks burned as I reminded myself that I was working for Griff, and the only reason I was in his suite and his bed was because I was a total disaster the day before and had lost my keys. I wasn't his girlfriend or even one of the contenders. Olivia probably had a list a mile long of those already.

I might only be in the alien's suite in a professional capacity, but the fact remained that I was practically naked beneath the sheets. I had on my bra and panty set, but I'd draped my dress across the tufted bench at the foot of the bed so they wouldn't become any more of a wrinkled mess than it was already.

Glancing at it, I cringed. Wearing the same clothes to work would not be a good look, but what other choice did I have? I still didn't have the keys to my apartment, although I could get the building manager to let me in today, but not before I needed to be at work. My only hope was that my boss paid as little attention to me as I suspected she did. Regardless, I needed to get dressed before Griff finished his shower.

I swung my legs to the floor and tossed back the duvet, reluctant to leave the downy warmth. Just as I stood, the sound of the rushing water stopped.

"Frickety frack!" I was standing in the direct line of sight of the bathroom door, in nothing but a black lace bra and panties. This was officially the opposite of making a good, professional impression with a client.

There was no way I could get into my black dress in time, but I spotted a white robe hanging on the back of the partially closed door between the sitting room and bedroom. I made a dash for it as I heard Griff moving around in the bathroom. I pulled it from the hook and jammed my hands through the armholes like I was stabbing it, fumbling for the fabric belt and managing to tie it closed in front of me.

I was breathing heavily by the time I was fully covered by the robe, and I let out a relieved sigh that Griff hadn't walked out and seen my frenzy and lack of grace. I guess I'd overestimated how fast he would exit the bathroom, but that was better than being caught half naked in front of a client.

A knock on the door startled me, but I suspected that Griff might have ordered breakfast for us, since he'd watched me ordering the sandwiches the night before. I was dying for coffee, but I wouldn't have minded some of the crab cake eggs Benedict or French toast I'd seen on the room service menu. My stomach growled at the thought of a Plaza breakfast. How was I already this hungry after eating a plate full of fries before bed?

I padded through the sitting room and opened the door, expecting to see a room service waiter with a rolling cart. Instead, it was Olivia.

My mouth dropped open, and so did hers.

She held up her phone with the Find Your Phone app open. "It said you were at The Plaza, but I was sure that couldn't be right." She eyed me up and down. "What are you doing here?"

I opened my mouth to explain but her gaze left me, focusing on something behind me as her eyes grew so wide I thought they might pop out. I pivoted to see Griff walking from the bedroom with a towel slung low around his waist. Droplets of water trailed down his muscular chest and his washboard abs.

I lost the ability to speak for a moment, but Olivia found her voice.

"What the—?"

I jerked her inside the room before she could finish her question. "It's not what you think."

CHAPTER 15

Griff

The dark-haired woman I'd met the night before stumbled inside as Caroline slammed the door shut behind her. She gave me another pointed look, her gaze drifting to the fluffy, white fabric I'd wrapped around my waist. "What *do* I think?"

Caroline was wearing a white robe made from the same fluffy fabric, and she tugged the two sides closer together at her chest. "I didn't plan to end up in Griff's hotel room. I got a Lyft to go back to my place, but then Griff didn't like the look of the driver, so he got in with me."

"To ensure she arrived at her home safely," I added.

Olivia folded her arms over her chest as she listened.

"When I got to my place, I couldn't find my keys anywhere. They must have fallen out when I was cleaning out my bag at work, but my spare set was inside my apartment and the manager never answers calls at night. My only option was to sleep on the stoop or take Griff up on his offer to stay at his hotel."

"You could have stayed with me," Olivia said.

Caroline gave her a look. "And your forty moody roommates?"

Olivia shrugged and mumbled something about the word moody being too kind.

"Despite what it might look like now, we slept in different rooms, and nothing happened," Caroline said.

"That's almost a shame, considering how gorgeous this suite is." Olivia swiveled to take in the ice bucket and empty bottle, tilting her head at her friend. "You got a bottle of Dom and nothing happened? Now that really is a crime."

Caroline's cheeks tinged pink. "It was a gift from the hotel."

Olivia glanced between us and finally twitched her shoulders. "I guess I didn't think you'd have abandoned your boyfriend embargo so easily."

Boyfriend embargo? The two words seemed odd together, and I watched Caroline's cheeks color even deeper.

"What is a boyfriend embargo?" I asked, sweeping a hand through my wet hair so droplets trickled down the back of my neck.

"It's nothing," Caroline answered quickly. "It's not a real thing."

"It felt pretty real when you pledged not to get involved with another guy ever again." Olivia walked toward the coffee table as she eyed the empty plates. "Not that I blamed you. Your ex was a total jerk."

Caroline let out a strangled laugh. "I don't think I said ever."

"Oh, you definitely did."

Caroline wouldn't meet my eyes as her friend plopped down in a chair. I wanted to ask her to tell me about this jerk who had prompted a boyfriend embargo, but the way her hands held her robe tightly at her neck told me that she wasn't eager to talk more about it.

"Right now, we have bigger things to worry about." Olivia held up her device. "Have you checked your phone?"

Caroline's gaze darted to her bag on the floor. "Not since last night."

"Don't bother. I'll save you the time of reading all of Miranda's texts."

"Miranda texted me?" Caroline hurried over and snatched her bag from the floor.

"Actually, she texted both of us." Olivia twisted a dark strand of hair around one finger. "She saw the posts and pics."

Caroline retrieved her phone and gazed tentatively at the screen. "Is she upset?"

"Upset?" Olivia laughed. "She's thrilled. This is a public relations coup for Saks. Everyone is talking about the hot alien who came to find a bride for the holidays, and Saks Fifth Avenue is where he came to shop."

I shifted from one foot to the other and readjusted the cloth that was slipping down my hips. It was strange that the female was talking about me as if I wasn't standing in the room and dripping water onto the carpet. It wasn't a bad feeling to be called hot—I'd determined that hot was a good thing in the human realm—but my trip to Earth did not have anything to do with their strange, cold-weather holiday.

I opened my mouth to explain this, but Olivia continued. "Saks has put out a statement, no doubt written by Miranda, about how thrilled our elite personal shopping department, The Fifth Avenue Club, is to be the one chosen to find Griff the perfect bride just in time for the holidays."

"Of course, Miranda is using this to drum up business," Caroline said under her breath as she swiped her fingers across her screen.

Her friend leaned back and crossed her legs at the knees. "You have to admit it's a good marketing angle."

"As if we need more business." Caroline shook her head. "We're swamped as it is."

"At least it cements our positions and increases our chances of big Christmas bonuses." Olivia smiled brightly and winked at me. "I already told Miranda not to expect us in today because we're both going to be busy working with Griff."

Caroline's head snapped up. "She didn't push back?"

"Not a bit. She even offered to cover our clients for us."

I cleared my throat, causing a break in the fast-paced exchange between the two women. "I had hoped to keep my search for a mate quiet. I don't think I need two personal shoppers."

"Oh, sweetie." Olivia smiled at me and shook her head. "That ship has already sailed."

I instinctively tipped my head toward the sky. What ship?

"She means it's too late to keep things quiet," Caroline said with a sigh. "Now that it's on social media and there are pictures of you, there's no way to keep your search private."

She met my gaze, holding it as she gave me what almost seemed like an apologetic smile.

"And you one-hundred-percent need both of us working on this." Olivia stood and waved a hand at me. "How else would you know that you need to get dressed so you won't be late?"

"Late?" Caroline glanced at her. "Late for what?"

Olivia raised her brows. "His first date, of course."

CHAPTER 16

Caroline

"*How* ow does he have a date already?" I asked Olivia, as I stepped into the black dress I'd worn the day before, wobbling on one foot as I balanced on the other.

I'd grabbed my clothes from the foot of the bed so Griff could get dressed in the room where clothes had apparently been hung for him in the closet. The door between the spaces was closed, but I knew I didn't have long to change.

"Because one of us was busy scrolling through his new dating profiles while someone else was drinking champagne and sleeping in his bed." The look she gave me was unmistakable, but I still ignored it.

"Profiles?" I hoisted the dress up to my waist, then I shrugged off the robe and slipped my hands through the dress's sleeves. "As in plural?"

Olivia gave me a lazy shrug and handed me my red coat. "I wanted to cover all the bases. You never know if someone good might be lurking on one of the oddball apps."

I slid a side-eye glance at her. "Oddball apps?"

Now it was her turn to ignore my comment. "You're really going to wear the same clothes that you had on yesterday?"

I glanced down at slightly wrinkled dress. "It's not like I have a choice. You watched me leave a message for my building manager, but who knows when he'll be able to let me back into my place."

She bobbled her head back and forth as she appraised me, finally reaching behind her and untying the red scarf from her ponytail. She handed it to me. "Here. Tie this around your neck. At least the pop of color might make it look like a different outfit."

"Thanks." I took the silky scarf and wrapped it around my throat, tying it in a knot and tucking it down the front of my dress. I wasn't sure that anyone would believe that it was an entirely new outfit, but most of the pictures from the night before were dark, and I had a good feeling that people weren't focusing on me. They were interested in the blue alien who had an even better body than I'd imagined.

My mind went to Griff standing in a towel with water trickling down his bare skin. Even through his clothes, I'd suspected he was built, but the guy was literally all muscle. I remembered the cuts below his abs that ran in a V shape and vanished beneath the towel. I gave my head a soft shake to dislodge those distracting thoughts, blinking a few times when I realized that Olivia was staring at me with a bemused look on her face.

"I would say Earth to Caroline, but I have a feeling that what you're thinking about has nothing to do with our planet."

I huffed out a semblance of a laugh. "What?"

She cut her gaze to the door separating the sitting room from the bedroom and lowered her voice. "Are you sure there's nothing going on between you and Big Blue?"

I shook my head. "I'm sure, and don't call him that. It makes him sound like he belongs to Paul Bunyan."

"Fine, but I don't want to work my ass off setting up dates for him, if you're already riding the blue…"

I held up my palms as I cut her off. "I'm not. I promise."

Olivia eyed me for another second before grinning. "Okay, I believe you. If you'd gotten lucky last night, you'd be a lot cheerier. At least, I hope you would."

"I'm plenty cheery," I grumbled as I slipped my feet into my black pumps. Then I realized how ridiculous that sounded, and I joined my friend in laughing. "Okay, but would you be cheery if you'd been locked out of your apartment and were wearing yesterday's clothes?"

"That's literally every other Saturday night in my world."

I groaned and gave Liv a playful shove.

"At least you don't have to go into work doing the walk of shame. Miranda would never let you live it down."

I imagined that my boss wouldn't be impressed if she knew I'd stayed over in a client's hotel room, but I didn't intend for her to ever find out. If Olivia was right, Miranda would be so thrilled by all the publicity we were bringing Saks and her department, that she'd never threaten to fire us again.

"Now, are you ready to see Griff's first match?"

I'd almost forgotten the reason she'd shown up and insisted we get dressed. Any urge to laugh almost instantly evaporated.

Without waiting for an answer, Liv held up her phone screen. "She's twenty-three and a recent Columbia grad with a degree in anthropology, which I thought might be good."

"Why?" I asked, as I inspected the image of a woman who was pretty, if a bit heavily made up.

"If she studied anthropology, that means she must be interested in other cultures, right?"

I fought the urge to roll my eyes. "I guess."

Liv pulled the phone back and looked at the screen. "She seemed the least like an alien chaser of most of the profiles."

"How can you tell?" I hadn't used a dating app since before Ethan and I had gotten together, but I didn't remember any questions about where you stood on aliens.

"Just a feeling I get." Olivia slipped her phone in the pocket of her dress. "Besides, it's only the first date. Trust me, there are plenty of other possibilities."

My heart sank even though I didn't know why. This was what I wanted, wasn't it? I wanted Griff to find a match so he would be happy, and I wanted to keep my job and hopefully get a big Christmas bonus. Besides, Liv had been right about me swearing off guys. I wasn't even ready to date again, much less think about getting hitched.

I shuddered at the thought, stopping when the door opened, and Griff stepped into the room. Then my heart did a somersault, and I forgot how to breathe.

CHAPTER 17

Griff

I stepped from the car and took in the park filled with rows of transparent stalls surrounding a large oval, where people seemed to glide around in circles. Bare-branched trees rose into the slate gray sky overhead even though they didn't come close to reaching the heights of the city's buildings. I breathed in a potent blend of rich, savory scents and heady sweetness, as the air was also filled with laughter and shrieks of delight. "This is where humans have dates?"

Olivia led the way up cement steps and stopped, beckoning for Caroline and me to follow. "You can have a great date anywhere, but ice skating is the perfect Christmastime date."

"Ice skating?" I repeated the phrase that seemed so foreign to me. Ice was something to be avoided on a spaceship, and I had a hard time imagining that humans actually found it pleasurable to slide around on it, trying to stay upright.

"You'll love it," Olivia assured me, as she hurried forward and glanced at her device like she'd been doing every few moments.

"Or, if you're like me, you'll enjoy the hot cocoa afterward more," Caroline muttered as she walked beside me. She'd been quiet since I'd joined them after dressing, and I wondered what they had discussed that had made her have such a hard time holding my gaze. Even though we'd been sitting next to each other in the car ride over, she'd made an impressive effort to keep her leg from touching mine, which had meant that she'd practically sat on top of her friend.

"You do not go on ice skating dates?"

Caroline's pale hair was pulled up into a topknot, and it bobbled when she shook her head. "It's been a while since I've gone on a first date, but I try not to pick something where I'll both freeze and have the chance to break my tailbone."

I hesitated on the top step, and she turned to me with wide eyes.

"Not that you'd do that," she said quickly. "I'm sure you're much more athletic than I am. I mean, it's obvious you are..." Her cheeks turned pink, and she gave me a shaky smile. "What I mean to say is, I'm sure you'll be fine."

A steady stream of people drifted in and out of the various shops —some carrying aromatic food and beverages that steamed—and several did a double take when they saw me. I flinched at the raised devices pointed my way, even though I'd realized that the flat human tech they called phones contained no weapons.

"I do not know what to do on a human date," I told her in a low voice as we followed a few steps behind Olivia, reaching the low wall encircling the giant slab of ice.

"What do you do on dates on your world?"

"We do not date." I didn't want to tell her that our mates were usually selected for us at birth or why that had changed.

Her brows lifted slightly as she rubbed her gloved hands together briskly. "This is a chance for you to see if this particular woman has the qualities you'd like in a mate." She gave me a pointed look. "Whatever those are aside from being understanding."

I wanted to tell her that I had come up with more qualities to add to my list, but before I could, Olivia clutched my arm and yanked me toward her. "Griff, this is your date, Bethany."

A female with short brown hair curling from beneath a black knit cap smiled up at me. "Call me Beth."

"Beth," I repeated, noticing that this female was shorter than Caroline or Olivia even though she was already wearing unusual boots with blades on the bottom.

She followed my gaze to the ground. "I already put on my skates." She held up a massive pair of black boots with blades. "And I got these for you. I hope they fit."

Olivia held a hand up to her mouth and pretended to talk behind it. "I snuck a peek at your shoes, although there was no size written anywhere, so I guessed."

"I'm pretty sure Valorian shoe sizes aren't the same as U.S. ones," Caroline said, earning her a sharp look from her friend.

I took the odd boots. "Thank you."

My date motioned to a nearby stone bench, and I followed her, sitting down and exchanging my shoes for the skates.

"You're Valorian?" The woman asked, her voice high and chirpy as she constantly moved her head from side to side. "I've heard of Drexians but not Valorians."

"We are allies of the Drexians."

She nodded as if she understood the galactic implications of our alliance. "So you plan to return to your home world?"

I pushed myself to standing, surprised to find that it wasn't hard to balance on the blades. "Eventually I must, although I have spent most of my life traveling throughout the galaxy."

"That must have been amazing." She drew out the last word so that it was several long syllables as she stared at me with a look akin to reverence.

"It is all I have ever known."

We stepped our way toward the giant oval of ice as people moved to let us through.

"I have a confession to make," the female named Beth said before we stepped onto the ice. "I'm not very good at this. You might end up picking me up a lot."

"I do not mind picking you up." From what little I had read of human mating customs, I knew that males on dates were supposed to attend to the wishes of the females. I grabbed her around the waist and hoisted her under one arm as I stepped onto the ice, pushing off as she screamed as loudly as any of the other happy skaters around us.

CHAPTER 18

Caroline

"*A*m I losing my mind, or is Griff carrying her like she's a football?" Olivia slapped her hand over her eyes as we stood along the transparent barrier around the rink.

It wasn't hard to spot the enormous, blue Griff among the shorter humans gliding and swirling on the ice, and it didn't take more than a quick glance to see that he had the woman tucked under one arm as her arms and legs flailed. I put a hand over my mouth as giggles threatened to consume me.

"Are you laughing?" Olivia shot me a severe look. "This is a disaster."

I spotted lots of phones in the air and could only imagine how quickly these images would go viral. Then I remembered our boss who would be monitoring our progress with Griff and his search for a bride, and instantly sobered. "Sorry. You're right. Not funny."

I forced myself not to look at the couple on the ice again, because even though I knew it wasn't good for us, the sight of the woman shrieking and waving her arms and legs made it impossible not to laugh. "Hopefully, Beth will think it's funny. You know, like a cute story to tell their grandkids."

Olivia released an exasperated sigh before turning back to the rink and waving her arms over her head to get Griff's attention. "Put her down!"

I had to admit that a small part of me was pleased that the date was off to a rocky start, even though I was instantly ashamed of that thought. I should be trying to help Griff, not hope his attempts to find a nice woman failed. Helping him was what I'd promised to do, after all. I was still his personal shopper, even if I didn't have much of an idea of what he wanted.

I chanced a look at the rink and saw that Griff had put down his date. Her face was red, and her hat had fallen off, which meant her dark hair was a mess. Griff's expression was apologetic and pained, and I felt sorry for him.

Okay, Caroline. Do not be a crappy person and enjoy their misery. You've been on worse first dates.

I thought about the guy who'd insisted on bringing his ferret on a leash and the one who'd been late to the restaurant and then announced after we'd eaten that he'd forgotten his wallet. This wasn't worse than that, although I had the advantage that my bumpy first dates hadn't been posted online.

Beth looked like she was attempting to laugh it off, even though I could see from where I stood that she was annoyed and embarrassed. Still, she gave Griff a tight smile and held out her hand for him to take. Watching them hold hands and skate did something weird and unpleasant to my insides, so I looked away.

I breathed in, my stomach rumbling at the smell of cinnamon and grilled meat. I spotted a churro booth and burger place within easy reach. I hadn't eaten since the night before, and I was ravenous. Just as I was about to call out to Olivia, who'd moved a few feet down the barrier, if she wanted a churro, I froze at the sound of a familiar voice.

"Caroline?"

I stiffened, slowly turning to give myself time to plaster on a fake smile. "Hey, Ethan."

I hadn't seen my ex-boyfriend in months, which had been a great thing. Our breakup had not been even remotely close to a conscious uncoupling, and I'd seen from his posts online that he'd moved on impressively fast. But here he was, standing by himself and grinning at me as if we were best friends.

His brown hair was carefully spiked in the front, so it appeared causal, but I knew precisely how much time the prick spent perfecting his humble-even-though-I've-gone-to-prep-school persona. I remembered a time when I'd thought he was the best-looking guy in the world, but now his perfect smile and hazel eyes left me cold.

"What are you doing here?" I asked, peering around him for the equally preppy and perfect girlfriend I was sure must be some-where nearby. From what I'd seen on his Insta before I'd stopped looking, he went through a couple a month.

He shoved his hands deeper into the pockets of his charcoal gray, wool coat. "Actually, I'm here for you."

I barked out a laugh at this, and several people nearby glanced over. "Me? Why would you be here for me?"

"I've been thinking, Car. I think we made a mistake breaking up."

I stared at him, not even twitching at the fact that he'd used the nickname he knew I hated. "First of all, *we* didn't make a mistake. You broke up with me so you could sleep with other people."

"That's not exactly true." He frowned, cutting a nervous gaze around him. "We both needed space."

I held up a finger as my heart raced. "No, you needed freedom to bang your neighbor, and then you claimed you weren't ready to be serious because you needed to focus on work."

Irritation flashed across his face. Now that was the Ethan I remembered. He cleared his throat and the fake smile returned. "I did need time to focus on my work, but now that I have, I realize how great we were together."

"Were we?"

"Come on, Car." He stepped closer to me. "Don't be like that."

Now everything came rushing back—the way he manipulated every fight so that he was the victim and the way he twisted every story so that he was the good guy. I narrowed my gaze at him as my heartbeat steadied. Then my mind whirred with questions. "How are you here?"

"What?"

I pinned him with a hard gaze. "You said you're here for me, but how did you know I would be here?"

He glanced over my shoulder at the ice rink, and everything fell into place. Ethan knew how to find me because of Griff. He must have seen the pictures of me with Griff from the night before. If they were trending as hard as Olivia claimed they were, he couldn't have missed them. That's what this was all about. He'd seen me with another guy—a big alien—and he'd gotten jealous.

I had no doubt that images of me with Griff in Bryant Park had hit social media the moment we'd arrived, which had made it easy for Ethan to find me. I felt a wave of disgust that my ex only wanted what he thought he couldn't have and an even stronger sense of gratitude that he wasn't my boyfriend anymore.

"Let me make this easy for you, Ethan." I put a hand on his arm. "We were not a great couple, and we are never getting back together." He opened his mouth, but I cut him off. "It's not me, it's you."

I turned to walk away, but he grabbed my wrist and twisted me back to face him. His expression was contorted with anger, and his eyes were slits. "Are you seriously telling me that you prefer that blue monstrosity to—?"

His words died on his lips as his head tipped back and his jaw dropped. I didn't need to turn around to know that Griff was right behind me.

CHAPTER 19

Griff

*F*ury rippled through me like a crashing wave as I watched the man grab Caroline's arm and spin her to face him. I was already skating toward her position at the transparent wall encircling the rink, so it did not take me long to reach her. I released my hold on Beth's hand to step over the barrier directly behind Caroline.

"Are you seriously telling me that you prefer that blue monstrosity to—?"

The man's sneer died on his lips as he realized that I was looming behind her and over him. His mouth went slack as I folded my arms over my chest and pointedly looked at his hand on her arm. He quickly released her and stepped back. The human wasn't as foolish as he looked.

"Did I interrupt your conversation?"

Caroline shook her head as she smiled at me. "Not even a little bit. Ethan was leaving." She turned her back on the man, whose face reddened before he stalked away. "How was your first time ice skating?"

I watched the offending male's retreating back until he got lost in the crowd. Then I turned my attention fully to Caroline. "I do not understand why humans wish to strap blades to their feet to make it more difficult to stay upright."

"I get that. It's supposed to be fun, but I never found falling on my ass to be entertaining. Luckily for me, I have enough of an ass to cushion the landing."

My gaze drifted down to her ass, which was curvy and covered by her red coat, but it did not look as fluffy as a cushion.

She cleared her throat. "Where's your date?"

I swiveled my head at the reminder that the female I'd been skating with was still in the rink. "I do not know. She was beside me." I scanned the rink and spotted the dark-haired human heading off the ice with her hands fisted by her sides.

Caroline groaned. "It looks like she's leaving."

I followed her progress as she stomped away from us with Olivia chasing after her. "I do not think I was a very good date."

"I don't think she was too happy that you left her to come over here."

I pivoted back to Caroline. "He was touching you, and you didn't seem to like it."

"That's an understatement." She smiled at me. "Thanks for checking on me, but I was fine. I can take care of myself."

This didn't seem to be completely accurate, since she had been without a place to sleep the night before, but when she lifted her hands to her mouth to blow into them, I noticed they were trembling. I didn't know who the man was who had grabbed her, but she was more upset than she wanted me to believe.

"Is my first date over?" I asked. My feet hurt, and I was aware of the people eyeing me with curiosity.

"Chances are good, unless Olivia works some magic and convinces her to come back."

I remembered what the Drexians had told me about the human's holiday and the strange magic involved in the lore. I did not want Olivia to work any magic, especially if elves were involved. The female had been pleasant, but I had felt no warmth when I touched her, and she had not seemed pleased when I had tried to prevent her from falling by carrying her.

Caroline glanced around and then motioned to a bench. "I think it's safe for you to take off your skates."

I gratefully sank onto the hard seating and pulled off the black, bladed footwear, glad to slip my feet back into my regular boots. "My date mentioned that after you skate, you should drink heated chocolate."

Caroline smiled. "I wouldn't mind some hot chocolate."

I stood and held out my hand, which was not covered in thick fabric. Unlike humans, my skin didn't easily chill.

Caroline hesitated. "I don't think us holding hands would look great if Olivia does talk your date into returning."

I wanted to tell Caroline that I did not care how it looked. All I cared about was holding her hand until it stopped trembling.

Instead, I dropped my hand. "Is hand holding an important part of human dating?"

She lifted one shoulder as she started walking. "For some people." She snuck a glance at me. "You wouldn't normally hold hands with your personal shopper."

We walked side-by-side through the throngs of people until we reached a shop with glass walls and a sign over the entrance that read, "Max Brenner, Chocolate by The Bald Man."

Caroline led us inside, and I was instantly hit by a blast of heat and enveloped by the rich scent of sugar. Shelves were stacked high with colorful boxes, as people crowded around a glass-topped counter.

"Two small hot chocolates," Caroline said to a woman behind the counter and touched a plastic card to a device. Then she said to me, "I know you're a big guy, but it's so rich a small will be enough."

We didn't have to wait long before we were handed red-and-white paper cups that warmed my hand when I curled my fingers around one. Instead of leading us back outside, Caroline tugged me deeper into the shop, until we were edged in the farthest corner and hidden by a tall display of shiny, gold boxes. I instinctively angled my body so that only my back could be visible by anyone in the shop and Caroline would be completely blocked from view.

I watched Caroline take a sip of her drink, and I followed suit, allowing the rich chocolate to warm me as I swallowed.

"I am sorry I did not do well on my date."

She shook her head at me over the rim of her paper cup. "Don't sweat it. It was your first time."

"I am not sweating, but I am warm."

She laughed, and I noticed that her hands were no longer shaking as she cupped them around her beverage. "That's the hot chocolate. Isn't it amazing?"

"So far, this is my favorite part of ice skating."

"If you ask me, hot chocolate is always the best part of ice skating, or skiing, or sledding, or basically anything outside in the winter."

"Do I need to do any of those activities on my next date?"

Caroline's brows pressed together, and a line formed between her eyes. "You're still willing to go on more dates?"

"Well, I have not found a mate yet." I drew in a breath. "But now I know that I would like a mate who does not anger easily."

"I tell clients that sometimes we can determine what you like by first determining what you don't like." She cringed. "I'm guessing your date wasn't happy when you finally put her down?"

I flinched as I remembered the female's sharp tone as she'd glared at me. "She called me a big oaf."

"Ouch." She rested a hand on mine. "Don't let it bother you. She clearly wasn't the woman for you. Good thing for you Manhattan is filled with single women."

As the heat from her skin made my hand tingle, I realized that I did not want any of the other women in Manhattan. I wanted her.

CHAPTER 20

Caroline

*G*riff's expression changed. "I do not think I have time to date all the women in your city." Then, his gaze dropped to my hand resting on his.

I pulled it away and wrapped it around my paper cup, taking another sip of my decadently-rich hot chocolate and ignoring the buzzing of my fingertips. "You won't have to."

"Maybe I should not use your human algorithms to find a mate."

I didn't blame him for doubting the apps. I'd never met anyone good by swiping right, although I'd heard tales of couples meeting on Tinder and getting married. Well, maybe not Tinder, but one of the apps.

"It's hard to meet people," I told him, "especially in a city as big and crowded as New York. The algorithms are supposed to narrow down the field, but I don't know if that actually happens.

If you ask me, knowing that there is a world of possibilities—and all with profiles—makes it easier to keep looking. Back when you had to go to bars, there was more effort involved."

"We went to a bar."

I nodded. "True, but I'll bet most people there were meeting a Tinder date or just grabbing a cocktail."

"So, it is difficult to find a mate using an algorithm or visiting a bar?"

"Now you're catching on." When his brow furrowed, I quickly added. "But we'll find someone, I promise. Olivia is actually great at dating and tenacious. If anyone can find you the perfect woman, it's her."

Griff did not look convinced. "My first date was not perfect for me."

I thought about the pretty woman with the pixie haircut. "Was it just the fact that she snapped at you? Not that that isn't enough of a reason."

He cocked his head to one side. "I would also prefer a taller female. She was very small."

I remembered her tucked under his arm and stifled a grin. The alien was well over six feet tall. Maybe I wasn't the only one who found it annoying when tiny women dated huge guys. "How tall?"

He gave me a quick once over. "You are tall enough."

That was surprisingly nice to hear, since more than a few guys had found my height of five foot eight to be too tall, especially if I wore heels. Not that I'd given up heels for anyone or ever would. As far as I was concerned, guys with Napoleon complexes could suck it.

"This is good." I gave him an encouraging smile. "Our list for you is growing: understanding, slow to anger, and at least five foot eight."

Griff returned my smile, and I felt my insides warming even more than they had from the hot drink. Wait, was I vibrating?

It took me a moment to realize that my phone was going off in my pocket. I quickly retrieved it, glancing at the screen. "It's Olivia."

Not a huge surprise that she was searching for us, but I wasn't ready to be found, so I ignored her call. Instead, I opened my text messages and almost cheered. "My building manager messaged that he can let me in today." I noted the time. "But I need to leave now to meet him."

Griff drained the last bit of his hot chocolate. "Okay. I am ready to go."

I loved how quickly he'd assumed that he would be coming with me. "You should probably stay with Olivia. She might have convinced Beth to stay, and even if she didn't, she'll be on top of finding you the next woman to meet. Going with me downtown won't get you any closer to that."

He shrugged. "I would prefer to take a break from first dates."

I didn't blame him there. First dates were brutal, and I could only imagine how much worse it was if you didn't understand the culture or the idiosyncrasies of the language. I also felt a bit defensive of Griff and annoyed that his first date had called him an oaf. I hated mean girls, and the thought of Griff being treated badly by another woman who might be dating him for the wrong reasons triggered something in me.

I released a sigh. "Olivia is going to kill me for this, but okay." I held up a finger. "But only if you promise that we're going to work on adding more things to your list on the way."

He gave me a solemn nod and tilted his body forward in a partial bow. "I give you my word as Valorian."

I returned my gaze to my phone, tapping a quick response to my building manager to tell him that I was on my way. Then I shot off a rapid-fire text to Olivia, telling her that Griff wanted a break from his dates. I added that in the future he only wanted to meet women who were over five feet eight.

Rude, Olivia replied, which made me laugh since she was barely five feet four.

Before my friend could ask for our specific location, I turned off my phone so she couldn't track me and shoved it in my coat pocket.

"Follow me." I led Griff from the shop, ducking around the side of the building and winding through the crowds and stalls until we reached the street. I spotted a vendor selling scarves and hats, and I dug in my purse for some cash, before snagging a black wool scarf and handing the heavily bundled man behind the table a wrinkled bill.

I turned to Griff, stood on my tiptoes, and looped it over his head, covering his dark hair and wrapping it around the bottom half of his blue face. "This will help you blend."

As the black covered his head, a few flakes of snow drifted down and landed on it. I tipped my head up to see flurries falling from the slate-colored sky.

Griff held out his hands, his brow wrinkling as the snowflakes fell onto his skin and melted.

"Snow," I explained, my heart giving a little leap despite all my attempts not to let the holidays get to me. "We might have a white Christmas after all."

Then I waved down a Yellow Cab and beckoned for him to get in before we were spotted. Once we were both in and the cab was accelerating, I gave the cabbie my address and flopped back in the seat.

Griff pulled down the scarf from covering his mouth. "Are we running from someone?"

"More first dates," I said with a laugh, although I was only partially teasing. If I knew Olivia, she would have a slew of willowy women—all over five feet eight—lined up by the time we stepped from the cab. And I knew none of them would be good enough for him.

CHAPTER 21

Griff

*T*he smelly vehicle jerked to a stop on the same quiet street where we'd been the night before. There was more traffic, and the branches that had cast twisted shadows over the sidewalks were now bathed in light and dusted with white. Caroline hopped out and I followed, grateful to breathe in fresh air again. "I think I preferred Mr. Lyft's vehicle."

"The only reason we took a cab is so I could turn my phone off and not use the Lyft app." She cast a look at the yellow car as it sped away. "And too many people would spot you on the subway."

I had heard that the human city had transportation that ran under the ground like planet Mobu, with its maze of fast magnetic trains. I had also learned that the New York underground trains were not as pristine or lightning-fast.

Caroline hurried up the steps to her building, which were damp but not covered in white like the bushes to the sides. The tall, wooden door was wedged open, and she called out as she pushed it open. "Mr. Henry?"

A wiry man in a thick, green sweater emerged from a door behind the stairs. His white hair was as bushy as the tufts of hair over his eyes. "Good. You're here."

"I'm so sorry about all this." Caroline shook a few wet snowflakes from her hair as he trudged up the stairs in front of her and we followed. "Thank you for letting me in."

The man grunted as he stopped in front of the door on the third floor, wiggled a key in the lock, and pushed on the door to open it. "It happens." He let his gaze rest on me, and his unruly brows shot up.

I removed the scarf from my head and nodded at him, hoping that would reassure him. It didn't. He flattened himself against the wall as Caroline walked through the open door, seeming to hold his breath as I passed.

"Thanks again," Caroline called out, but the man was already stumbling down the stairs to get away.

"I do not think he liked me."

Caroline waved this off as she closed the door. "Don't worry about him. He's old. Not all of the older generation is open to the idea of aliens."

Now that I was inside her dwelling, I paused to take it in. No wonder she'd been impressed by the size of my hotel room. Her apartment was a fraction of its dimensions.

She quickly started straightening items stacked on the table by the door. "Sorry about the mess. I didn't think I'd have company."

"It is not messy," I said, glancing at the cooking area extending to one side of the entrance that would barely hold two individuals standing side by side, "but it is small."

She laughed. "Well, it's New York. An efficiency here would be a closet in the Midwest."

"I am accustomed to small living spaces, but that is because I've lived on spaceships." I followed her into the room that held a pair of stuffed chairs facing a flat screen and a low table covered in paper. "I thought that Earth would have larger dwellings on its surface."

"We do." She shrugged off her coat and tossed it on the back of one of the purple chairs. "In Texas—or Brooklyn."

I swiveled my head to take in the bed that was tucked into a nook to one side of the living area, noting the colorful drawings covering the walls that were similar to the black-and-white ones scattered on the low table. "Did you draw the art on your walls?"

She slid a brief glance at the wall. "It's a hobby of mine. I even considered going to art school, but art degrees don't take you far, so I made my parents happy and majored in marketing."

"And now you shop for people."

She met my gaze for a beat and held it. "Working at Saks isn't a forever job for me. It's a steppingstone."

"What is your forever job?"

She huffed out a breath. "You ask a lot of questions."

"There is a lot about Earth I do not understand." I did not say the truth, which was that she intrigued me. She was a beautiful female who, according to her claims, did not want a mate. She worked at a place she considered temporary, but she didn't know what she would rather do. Her living space was covered in her art, which displayed undeniable talent, but she only considered it a hobby.

"I'm dying to take a shower and change into clothes I haven't been wearing since yesterday. Can I leave you out here and trust you not to burn the place down?"

I didn't know how I would ignite a fire, but I nodded. She walked past the bed and through a door that I assumed was the bathing chamber, closing it behind her.

I took a few steps toward the windows that looked over the street and peered down. Cars drove past and people strode along the sidewalk with small animals on leads, despite the white snow fluttering in the air. I preferred this slower environment to the bustling area with the skating rink, even if it was more modest in every way than Valoria.

The sound of rushing water drew my attention back to the inside of the apartment, and my mind couldn't help wandering to the female bathing. It was not lost of me that I had spent more time with the person who was supposed to be helping me find my perfect match than I had with any other female since I'd come to Earth.

Since I'd met Caroline, it had been hard to think about any other female. Not only had she been with me the entire time, but we also seemed to be taking turns saving each other. I'd saved her from the fate of having no place to sleep. She'd saved me from having to continue with my awkward date. Now she was saving me from having to withstand more dates. I thought about walking up to her and the man who'd called me a blue monstrosity. I sensed that I'd interrupted something more than a casual conversation, and maybe saved her from something less pleasant than an unwanted hand on her arm, but she hadn't mentioned him since.

"Now, I feel human again." Caroline emerged in a cloud of scented steam with a swath of fluffy, pink fabric wrapped around her chest. Her pale hair was piled up on top of her head, and wet tendrils dripped water down her neck. She paused when she saw me standing by the window. "I guess that was a weird thing to say. I don't know what it would feel like to be another species."

I opened my mouth to tell her that she hadn't offended me, but my throat wouldn't work as I watched her pull clothing from a small closet, and I tried desperately not to stare at her long legs and instead remind myself that she could not be the one.

CHAPTER 22

Caroline

I emerged from the bathroom again after changing into black yoga pants, a purple tank top, and a long gray cardigan, and I padded barefoot across the wooden floor. "Now I really feel like a new woman."

Griff was sitting in one of my chairs facing the TV, which was turned off. He hadn't spoken since I'd showered and changed, and I wondered if he was startled seeing me in casual clothes. After all, I'd been in business attire and heels since he met me.

"The hot chocolate was delicious, but since I didn't eat breakfast, I'm still starving." I glanced at the wall clock as I stepped into the galley kitchen. "Can you believe it's already afternoon?"

I opened the refrigerator door and peered inside. Just as I'd suspected. A few containers of Chinese takeout of questionable age, condiments lining the doors, a few bottled cold brews, and a roll of sugar cookie dough with snowflakes on the package. At least the holiday detailing told me the cookie dough was fresh. "I know it's not a real meal, but how do you feel about cookies? It would be in keeping with our sugar theme for the day."

I grabbed the roll of cookie dough and straightened as I closed the door, yelping when I saw Griff standing directly on the other side.

"I did not mean to scare you."

I put a hand to my heart, which was pattering unevenly in my chest. "It's fine. You move stealthily for a big guy, that's all."

"I am unfamiliar with cookies, but I trust you."

I almost dropped the dough. "What do you mean you're unfamiliar with cookies? You've never baked cookies, or you've never eaten them?"

"I have done neither."

I pointed the long roll at him. "Now, that is a crime."

His blue eyes widened for a beat, but I shook my head quickly. "Not a real crime. That's just an expression."

"Your language has many expressions that don't mean what they mean."

I laughed as I thought about it. "I guess it does." I retrieved a small cookie sheet from the drawer under my rickety oven, the metal creaking as I closed it.

"The cookies are in that food tube?" Griff asked as I put the roll of dough on the counter.

"The dough is, but we need to bake it." I bobbled my head as I reconsidered this. "We *should* bake it."

"Much of the food on our spaceships comes in tubes, so maybe cookies are not very different from the nutritional pastes we eat on long voyages."

I wrinkled my nose. "This is definitely not a food paste, and its nutritional value is highly debatable."

The alien watched me as I pulled out a wooden cutting board, used a paring knife to cut a slit down the seam of the cookie roll, and peeled off the plastic. I eyed the cold cylinder of dough. "We could slice it and bake it like that, but that's not very festive, and I'm not as much of a Scrooge as Olivia thinks I am."

"Cookies are supposed to be festive?"

As much of a grump as I'd been about Christmas since working at Saks, I couldn't resist telling him about the best parts of the season. "They aren't always, but when you bake cookies around the holidays, you usually make them a bit special. When I was a kid there were certain cookies we only made at Christmas, and I waited all year to eat them."

"Is there a rule that you can only eat them at one time of the year?"

I shook my head, grinning at his legitimate question. "No, but that's just the way it was. My mother only made ginger molasses or peanut butter kiss cookies in December, which was why baking cookies was one of my favorite holiday memories."

He glanced at the cream-colored dough. "Are we making special cookies?"

I frowned as I opened the cabinets, searching until I spotted a glint of shiny metal poking from inside a dented loaf pan. I pulled it out and held the snowflake shaped cookie cutter in the air. "Now they're special."

He looked a bit confused as I scooted around him and positioned him in front of the cutting board. "Technically, we should roll out the dough, but we're going to cheat." I handed him the knife, "You're going to cut them in slices and then I'll use the cookie cutter to make them festive."

He eyed the roll, finally lifting the knife and bringing it down in a fast, hard stroke onto the cutting board. A slice of dough about an inch wide plopped from the roll.

I gave my head a quick shake. "Well, that's one way to do it." I moved the dough over on the cutting board so that it was flat and cut it into a snowflake, which I then moved to the cookie sheet.

Reaching carefully for the knife, I closed my hand over his and gently guided it down to the dough roll, slicing through without using a violent hacking motion. "Try it this way."

He made a face which told me that he thought his way was better, but he did cut the next slice less violently. We worked quietly side by side for a few minutes, until I could feel Griff's gaze on me.

I stopped and swung my head to meet his probing gaze. "What?"

"What is a Scrooge?"

I almost laughed at his question. "Where did that come from?"

"You have mentioned the word before, and you said that your friend believes you to be one. My universal translator implant does not know it."

I blew out a breath. "It means that I don't like Christmas, which isn't true."

He curious expression didn't waver. "So, you do enjoy the holiday?"

"I usually do, but I guess I don't as much this year." I'd tried to tell myself that it was only because of my high-maintenance clients, but that was a lie. "My family always made a big deal about Christmas, but I'm not going home this year, so it doesn't feel the same."

"Why are you not returning home?"

I focused on peeling a cut-out dough snowflake from the cookie cutter. "My parents think I made a big mistake in breaking things off with Ethan, the guy you met at the rink. They were convinced we'd get married and have the perfect family, just like them, and they blamed me when things ended. I got tired of their questions about him every time I called, so I stopped calling and started dodging their calls. It seemed weird to go home after not talking for months."

"He is not good enough for you."

I pivoted to smile at Griff. "Thanks. How is it that you picked up on that in two minutes and they never did?" I shook off that thought. "Anyway, I guess I'm sad that I'm alone at the holidays, which is why I've been trying to ignore them, which is impossible in this city."

"You are not alone."

"I know, I know, but Liv isn't as into ugly sweaters and gag gifts as you might think."

His blue eyes held mine, and I was suddenly aware of our shoulders touching. Griff's little finger brushed mine on the counter, sending frissons of heat up my arm.

"I did not mean Olivia."

The galley kitchen seemed overly warm as my breath hitched in my throat. "Who did you—"

Before the rest of the question could leave me, Griff had dropped the knife and his hands were raking through my hair and pulling my lips to his in a claiming kiss that turned my knees into jelly.

CHAPTER 23

Griff

I'd been imaging how her lips would taste since I'd watched her sipping her hot beverage so delicately, and her curvy, pink mouth was every bit as intoxicating as I could have dreamed. The rich taste of chocolate lingered on her tongue, but I suspected the real sweetness was all her.

She moaned into my mouth as I parted her lips with my tongue, and the sound sent heat ricocheting through me. I fisted her soft, damp hair in my fingers to hold her head to mine as I devoured her mouth, but then I needed to feel more. I released my grip on her hair and let my hands move swiftly down her back, spanning her body with my broad palms and letting the tips of my fingers brush the sides of her breasts.

When she emitted a hungry sound and arched into me, my cock strained painfully against my pants. Instead of pulling away at the hardness pressing into her, Caroline lifted her hands to my head and scraped her fingers roughly through my hair. Then she gave a little hop and wound her legs around my waist.

Even though her movement took me by surprise, I caught her and held her by the ass as she slid her hands to the side of my face and kissed me deeper. I staggered from the narrow cooking area and took uneven steps to the bed as she tugged my shirt from my pants.

When I paused at the foot of it, she tore her mouth from mine and pulled my shirt over my head. She quickly shrugged her own long sweater off her shoulders and dropped it to the floor. Her eyes were burning, and her chest heaved as she ran her hands across the muscles of my chest, scraping her fingernails gently so that she left dark trails in my blue flesh for a beat. "More."

The single word almost made my legs buckle, but I maintained a shred of control. As much as I wanted her with every throbbing fiber of my being, I did not want her to regret anything. "You are sure?"

She nodded as she ran her trembling fingers through my hair and rocked her body into mine. "I need this."

As much as I wanted the words to convince me, I hesitated. "Do you need this, or do you need me?"

She blinked a few times as she drew in ragged breaths. "You. I need you."

"Why?" I rasped, even as I lowered her onto the bed and braced my arms on either side of her.

Caroline bit the edge of her bottom lip as her gaze locked onto mine. "Because you're kind and thoughtful, and you make me feel safe. Oh, and you make me forget to breathe."

"Not because I am an alien?"

She tilted her head. "I kind of forgot you were."

That stopped me, but then I realized that I'd forgotten that she was alien to me. I'd stopped noticing how different she was from Valorian females.

"What about me?" she asked as I brushed a strand of hair from her face. "Do I check off everything on your list?"

I thought about the foolish list I'd brought to Earth before I knew anything about the planet's females or culture. I'd thought that I would care about things like tentacles or the number of breasts, but none of that mattered to me now. I couldn't even remember everything that I'd put on my long list.

I gazed at Caroline with her pale hair fanned out on the bed behind her, her green eyes wide, and her lips pink and plumped from my kisses. Her shoulders were bare except for the thin fabric straps from her top, which scooped low to expose her creamy cleavage. It struck me that no other female had stood a chance from the moment she'd banged her head and emerged from beneath her desk and then hopped awkwardly on one leg as she'd attempted to put on her shoe. I'd been intrigued and then charmed even as she'd made a complete fiasco of finding me a bride. "You *are* the list."

Her eyes widened, and her lips opened in surprise.

"You are what I want." I lowered my head and feathered a kiss across her mouth. "I did not know what I truly wanted in a female until I met you. You are beautiful and honest and patient, and I do not believe you are a Scrood."

"Scrooge," she said with a giggle.

I lifted my head back up to meet her eyes. "Or that."

Her brow furrowed. "But I'm your personal shopper. I'm supposed to find you the perfect bride. I'm definitely not supposed to do this."

"I do not need you to find me anyone else. You are perfect for me."

"But all those women who matched with you, your ice-skating date, all the publicity about Saks fulfilling your holiday wish list." She bit her lip again, this time harder. "Olivia would kill me, and Miranda would fire me."

"None of that matters" My heart beat rapidly as my chest swelled. "I will protect you. A Valorian always protects his mate to the death."

"Mate?" Her voice was little more than a whisper.

I dipped my head to nip at the soft skin of her neck, prompting a breathy moan to escape from her lips as she arched into me. "My perfect mate."

Caroline's body stilled, and her rapid breathy stopped. "Do you hear that?"

I'd heard little but the rushing of blood in my ears, but now that she was rigid, I sat back and listened. A buzz of voices was drifting from outside the window, which was odd considering how quiet her street had been when we arrived. Then a sharp rap at the door made us both jerk.

"It must be the building manager again." Caroline frowned as we both sat up. "Olivia doesn't know we're here, and I turned my phone off so she couldn't track us."

"I will tell him to go away." I strode to the door, ignoring my shirt crumpled on the floor as Caroline stood up and walked to the window.

Just as I yanked open the door prepared to tell the man that he should not disturb us, Caroline gasped from behind me. "Don't!"

But it was too late. I'd already thrown back the door to a faceless man with a device pressed to his eye. He unleashed a barrage of clicking sounds as he called out Caroline's name. I slammed the door closed as quickly as I'd opened it, turning slowly around to see Caroline's stricken face as she took in my bare chest.

She sank onto a chair with her head in her hands. "The street is crawling with paparazzi. How did they find us?"

I did not understand the word paparazzi, but from Caroline's slumped shoulders, I knew it was not good.

CHAPTER 24

Caroline

I didn't need to see the images in the paparazzi's camera to know exactly what they looked like. Griff was shirt-less, and I had on a skimpy tank top with one strap hanging off my shoulder while my hair was no doubt a tousled mess.

I shook my head as I held it in my hands. "Olivia is going to murder me."

"How will your friend know?"

I peeked at him through my fingers without sitting up. "That photographer isn't going to waste any time selling those images to the highest bidder, which means they'll be online in minutes and Olivia will see them. She never misses anything online. I'm pretty sure she has a direct TMZ download into her brain."

Griff looked like he hadn't understood half of what I was saying. I huffed out a breath. As irritated as I was, I couldn't be angry with him. None of this was his fault. He'd just had the bad luck to get me as a personal shopper when he'd walked into The Fifth Avenue Club. It wasn't his fault that he'd gotten stuck with a walking disaster.

"That man took images of us to display for public viewing?" He swiveled toward the door as if he might barrel through it and chase down the photographer.

"I don't know how he got in the building." Then a dark thought swirled in my brain. Had the building manager given us away? No one else knew where we were.

"Should I eject him?"

I glanced at Griff, still huge, blue, and shirtless. I had a feeling when he said eject, he didn't mean he would hurry the man down the stairs. I envisioned a body catching air as it was tossed from the building. "No. I don't want you to get in trouble. That would only make things worse."

I stood and walked to the window, pulling back the sheer drape and darting a glance outside. The sidewalk remained crowded with photographers and news vans were double-parked in the street, although it had stopped snowing. Below me, a woman poked her head from her window and waved her cell phone at the prowling paparazzi. "I don't know why you're here, but I've called the cops."

I exhaled so loudly I was almost surprised my downstairs neighbor didn't hear me and turn. The woman had impressive hearing and had scolded me more than a few times for walking noisily above her. For once, having her scrutinize everyone and everything was coming in handy. "Thank you, Mrs. Davenport," I said aloud even though she couldn't hear me through my closed window. "Finally having a self-appointed building monitor has paid off."

I pulled back and let the sheers fall. Then I made a beeline for my purse and dug my phone from it. I knew exactly who would know what to do. I dialed and held the phone to my ear.

"Caroline? What the hell?"

I was so relieved to hear Olivia's voice I didn't even recoil from her shrill tone. "I know, I know."

"I thought Griff was taking a break around Bryant Park, but now you're at your place, and you're half naked? Caroline, what the—?"

"It's not what you think," I said hurriedly, avoiding Griff's gaze as he stood looking at me from across the room. "Yes, we came back to my apartment, but only because I needed the building manager to let me in since I lost my key. Then I had to change because I'd been in the same clothes since yesterday."

"Yeah, the scarf didn't really do much to help with that," she admitted. "That doesn't explain why Griff is barely dressed."

I cringed. Like I suspected, she'd seen the photos, but they'd gone up even quicker than I imagined. "His shirt got dirty, that's all."

Olivia made a disbelieving sound in her throat, and my face warmed. I was glad she wasn't there to see me blush because then she'd know I was lying. She'd always claimed that I was a crap liar.

"Where are the pictures?"

"Everywhere." She sighed. "Listen, babe, this is not great."

I rubbed a hand over my forehead as I snatched my gray cardigan from the floor and put it on while bracing the phone to my ear with my shoulder. "You don't think Miranda has seen the pics, do you?"

"Maybe not yet, but she will." The sound of traffic surrounded Liv wherever she was, and she raised her own voice to compensate. "We need to do damage control."

I picked up Griff's shirt that was crumpled on the floor and handed it to him without meeting his gaze. "Okay, how do we do that?"

"I'm not a PR expert, but in this case, I don't think making a statement would do much good. First off, Miranda likes to be the one to make the statements, and you and I are too far down the Saks pecking order to be issuing anything official."

"It wouldn't have to be official. It could just be a statement from Griff saying that the pictures are inaccurate."

"No good. There have been too many photos of you and Griff together already and now one of you two barely dressed in your apartment? Only an idiot would believe that it's completely innocent and you're just his personal shopper."

My cheeks burned at this. Griff had told me that he didn't want me to keep looking for a wife for him, which meant that I technically wasn't working for him anymore. My mind went to everything else he'd told me, and my pulse spiked. Had he been serious when he'd told me that I was what he wanted, or was it just the heat of the moment making him say what he thought I wanted to hear?

After being manipulated by Ethan's empty promises and sweet talking for two years, I didn't know if I was the best judge of what it sounded like when a guy was being honest. I wanted to believe that Griff was different and that he wasn't lying to get into my pants, but doubt teased the back of my brain and told me that I was the last woman who would ever be able to judge something like that.

"What we need is an alternate narrative," Olivia said.

A police siren blared a few warning blasts outside, and I heard the sound echoing through the phone. "Meaning what?"

"Griff's visit to New York has exploded on social media. Everyone knows why he's here and is speculating on what type of woman he'll pick. We've already given them one option, although just between you and me, Beth is a hard no. Still, people don't know that yet. We need to give them another dating option to distract from you."

"Another date?" I ignored Griff's stormy expression as he folded his arms across his bare chest and held his shirt in his hand without making any move to cover his impressive physique.

"If we blanket the press with pics of him on another date, the few photos of you will be buried, hopefully before Miranda gets wind of them."

Not only did I know that Griff would not go along with it, I despised the thought of him on another date. I might not know how serious he'd been when he'd said he wanted me, but I hadn't been lying when I'd told him I was into him. The problem was, being with Griff meant more than just a fun Christmas fling. He was looking for a wife, and I was still healing my wounded heart.

"What about you?" I suggested. "You could pretend to date him."

"Miranda would love that. Two of her employees violating her cardinal rule of no dating the clients?" She let out a hard laugh. "Now buzz me up."

"What?" I walked to the window, spotting her standing directly below me on the top step of the stairs leading into my building.

"The cops aren't letting anyone in." Olivia waved a red-gloved hand at me. "And the lady from the second floor is giving me the stink-eye."

I hung up as I left the window and crossed to the door, pressing the button on the wall. I turned to face Griff and found him standing so close he was almost touching me.

"I told you that I do not wish to go on anymore dates." He raised a hand to brush a strand of hair from my face. "I have found you."

My stomach lurched. How did I tell him that he didn't want someone as wounded as me?

CHAPTER 25

Griff

"*I* told you that I do not wish to go on anymore dates." She stood with her back to the door and her head tipped up to meet my gaze. I brushed a stray golden lock of hair from her face. "I have found you."

Caroline's mouth opened and closed, reminding me of the gilly beasts on Paranthan Five who took in air through their sucker mouths, although she was much more attractive than the green-skinned creatures. Staring at her pink lips made me want to crush my mouth to hers again, and I cupped her chin in one hand and dragged my thumb across her full bottom lip as I lowered my head.

"This is a bad idea." She ducked under my arm and twisted so that she was standing behind me.

I spun around to face her, her words like a cold blast of water dousing my heat. "Why? I have told you that you are perfect for me and everything I want."

She shook her head and dropped her gaze to the floor. "I'm not. Trust me."

How could I trust her when it came to my own desires? Did she think I had been lying when she was beneath me on the bed? "I meant every word I said to you when we were—"

"About that." Caroline interrupted me. "We can't let Olivia know that anything happened. Not that anything did happen, but that anything was about to happen or could have happened even though it definitely didn't."

Her rush of words confused me. This was not the same woman who had been desperately tearing at my shirt and raking her fingers through my hair. What had happened?

"Caroline." I closed the small distance between us and grasped her hands. "There is no need to worry. I will explain everything to your boss. You will not get reprimanded for what has happened between us."

She snatched her hands from me. "That's right because nothing has happened." She finally looked up with pleading eyes. "It can't."

A strange lump lodged in my throat. "Why not?"

She dragged a hand viciously through her hair. "You don't want me. I'm not what anyone would consider available."

Ice slid through my veins. "You already have a mate?"

Was it the male from the ice rink, the one who'd looked at me like he wished his eyeballs could shoot photons? Caroline's stiff shoulders had told me she did not enjoy his company, but maybe she was right, and I understood human females even less than I'd thought.

"I don't have a mate." She exhaled loudly. "I doubt I'll ever have one. Some people just aren't made for marriage."

This sounded wrong to me. Valorians all took mates, at least we had before we'd lost so many of our females. Why would someone as desirable and kind as Caroline believe that she would not make a good mate? I studied her pained expression. "Did someone tell you this?"

She looked away, her jaw tight. "Marriage requires sacrifice and overlooking your partner's faults and betrayals. I wasn't willing to do that." Her voice was robotic as if she were repeating someone else's words. "I couldn't. I guess I'm not that tough."

I had never heard anyone talk of overlooking betrayals in a mate. Why would one mate betray the other? I stepped closer to her. "I would never betray you."

Caroline swung her head so she locked eyes with me, her gaze glassy. "Maybe you wouldn't. You aren't human, after all. Maybe Valorian males don't screw around like human ones do."

Hot fury pulsed through me. "Did someone betray you?"

She barked out a mirthless laugh. "It doesn't matter. I got over it, but it made me realize that I'm not built for marriage." She gnawed at the corner of her lip. "I'm sorry if I led you on or made you think I was a possibility."

This didn't make any sense. It hadn't been long ago that she'd been telling me how much she needed me. Those words I'd believed. They'd been real and raw. These words were lies she'd taught herself to believe, but they held no truth. I'd seen a glimpse of the fiery woman inside who was hungry for connection and hungry for me.

But Caroline believed the lies. I would not force her to accept me or take something that she did not freely give. I steeled myself for the pain that washed over me as I took a step back. "I am also sorry."

She opened her mouth again, regret wrinkling her brow, but a hard rap behind us precluded whatever she would have said to me. Her gaze went to the door, and she pushed past me to open it. "Liv!"

Her friend stood with her hands on her hips and a blue wool cap partially covering her dark hair. Olivia's gaze traveled to me, still bare-chested, and then to Caroline's tousled hair. "Still a disaster, I see."

Caroline threw herself in her friend's arms. "I'm so glad you're here. This is a mess."

Olivia patted Caroline's back, as her brows pinched together in confusion. Then she looked at me, cocking her head to one side. "Did I miss something?"

"She is upset that—" I started to explain but Caroline reared back.

"We can't leave because of all the paps downstairs," Caroline said quickly, shooting me a warning look over her shoulder.

The door across the hall opened to reveal a hulking figure in a glittery red dress with white trim and matching high-heeled shoes with toes that curled up. His head was bald until he tugged on fake white curls topped with a red and white pointed hat. "You can go out the back using my fire escape."

CHAPTER 26

Caroline

I took in Carl's outfit, his merry attire instantly banishing the feeling of panic that had welled in my throat. "Do you have a show today?"

Since this was New York, I wasn't exceptionally close with my neighbors, but Carl was my favorite. Aside from exchanging the usual pleasantries and occasionally swapping milk for coffee, he'd asked my opinion on wig styles and for assistance zipping him into gowns, which was how I'd learned that he performed as a drag queen on the side.

He straightened his wig and gave me a wink, his false lashes fluttering over glittery green eyeshadow. "You know it. Once a day leading up to Christmas, with our big show on Christmas Eve."

"You look amazing." I'd seen my across-the-hall neighbor in plenty of fabulous costumes in the time I'd lived in the building, but his Mrs. Claus outfit might have been my favorite.

Olivia cleared her throat, pulling me back to reality.

"Sorry, Liv. This is Carl, my neighbor. Carl, this is my best friend Olivia and," I hesitated over the right word as I glanced at the blue, bare-chested alien, "my client Griff."

Carl gave Liv a finger wave and Griff a very slow once-over. "Mmmhmm. Sure he is, sweetie." He put a hand to one side of his mouth and spoke in a stage whisper. "I've seen the photos online."

My face warmed, but I rolled my eyes. "It's not what it looks like."

"That's my line, doll."

I ignored Carl's wicked grin and his deep-throated laugh. "You said you can get us out the back way?"

He spun on one heel and waved for us to follow him inside his apartment, jingling as he went. "Ida is picking me up in the back alley in a few. I doubt you'll run into many photographers out there."

I dashed past Griff, grabbed my purse and the black flats that happened to be strewn near my couch and ran back across the hall, pulling the befuddled alien with me. Liv closed my door and we all traipsed into my neighbor's place.

Olivia glanced at Griff once we were standing in the even smaller and more crowded apartment. "There may not be the same crowds in the back, but you'll need to put on that shirt."

Carl pivoted back around to face us. "Oh, I don't know about that. If you really want to be incognito, I'd lose the uniform." He spread his long arms wide, motioning to the racks of spangled and glittery clothing lining the walls. "They'd never recognize you in one of my costumes."

Liv ran a hand along the clothes. "Carl is right. No one would think for a moment that Griff was part of a group of drag queens."

I stole a glance at Griff, expecting his face to be etched with horror. It wasn't. He was appraising the outlandish clothes with the same curiosity he'd given to my drawings, but there was none of the gruff judgment I would have expected from someone so tough and masculine. Ethan would have never even walked into Carl's place.

Another reason to be glad you're not with him.

"Will any of your clothes fit me?"

I swung my head to Griff as he questioned Carl. The muscular Mrs. Claus studied him for a beat before nodding.

"You're taller than me, hon, but we've got a similar build." Carl nudged him in the ribs. "Lucky us, am I right?" Then he pulled a red and white striped sequined dress from the rack. "You would make a divine Candy Cane."

I fully expected Griff to balk at the idea of wearing a long dress with fluffy white feathers rimming the neckline. Instead, he nodded and started to unfasten his pants.

I grabbed Griff's hands to stop him, although Carl's eyes were already saucers. "Why don't you change somewhere more private?"

Carl muttered something about me being a spoilsport, but he flapped a hand at the open bathroom door, the bells around his cuffs jingling. "You can dress in there while I doll up the girls."

Griff disappeared into the bathroom carrying the candy cane dress, and Olivia turned to me. "You know I love a good hare-brained scheme, but if Miranda finds out that we dressed our client in drag—"

"She won't find out." I patted Liv's arm. Even if anyone saw us, they'd never believe their own eyes. What kind of personal shoppers from Saks would dress their client like a giant sequined candy cane? Not ones that wanted to keep their jobs, I thought as I swallowed hard.

Carl thrust a gold lamé cocktail dress with heavy black fringe around the hem at me. "You can be a lamp shade, darling."

I looked longingly at the collection of long gowns with fur trim then back at the shiny dress. "A lamp shade?"

He eyed my yoga pants. "I know you've got great legs even if you never show off your stems to their full potential. Besides, the hat will cover your hair, which is a dead giveaway." He swiveled to Olivia and snatched a long, green, ruffled number with colorful ball ornaments sewn onto the fabric. "You will be a Christmas tree."

She eyed the full length dress and the pointed hood with a star at the tip. "What about my legs?" He narrowed his gaze at her, and she shrugged. "Fine. It's not like I have to wear this for long."

"You dress while I gather the rest of my props." Carl ducked into the alcove sleeping area that mirrored my own floor plan.

Liv and I quickly shed our clothes and slipped into the dresses. Mine was baggy at the top and belled out at the bottom thanks to a hoop in the hem, which made me look very much like a lampshade. Liv's dress covered her from head to almost toe, and when she pulled up the hood, only her face peeked from the stiff, green ruffles.

"Well, Jingle my balls." Carl sucked in a breath as he emerged from the sleeping area holding a tote bag over one arm. "You two look good enough to put on stage."

"I think you mean jingle your bells," I said as he added a gold hat to my head, the black fringe hanging over my face.

"I don't think he did," Liv muttered from beneath the ruffles.

I parted the fringe covering my eyes to pin Carl with a hard look. "No stage. We appreciate you helping us, but we aren't performing."

"Fine." He huffed out a breath, then he emitted a strangled sound as Griff walked from the bathroom sheathed in red and white sequined stripes that seemed to mold to his muscles. The feathers around the neckline covered the bottom half of his square jaw, but his blue eyes locked onto me.

Even in a form-fitting dress that left little to the imagination and highlighted every ridge and bulge, Griff was the hottest guy I'd ever seen. If I'd been a working lamp taking in his impossible-to-miss bulge, I would have shorted out just looking at him.

"I don't normally like peppermint," Carl sighed, "but I'd lick—"

The beep of a car horn made us all jump, and Carl ran to the back door as he snatched the clothes we'd taken off and jammed them into a paper shopping bag. "Come on, our ride's here!"

Liv followed Carl while I brought up the rear with Griff. Once we'd closed the door behind us and were on the metal fire escape, Griff slid his gaze to me.

"You look beautiful."

I laughed and shoved the fringe from my eyes. "Not as good as you."

The blue of his cheeks darkened. "I hope this works to keep you out of trouble."

As I turned to look at him, my toe caught on the open weave of the metal escape, and I stumbled. "You're doing this for me?"

He caught me, his strong arms wrapping around me. "I would do anything for you."

His words were so honest and direct that I lost my ability to speak, and I fought to urge to sink into the warmth of his embrace and never leave. But I remembered myself and straightened, forcing myself to head for the stairs, grateful that this fire escape wasn't one of the rickety kinds with dangling ladders.

Maybe I'd been wrong about him. Griff wasn't human, so how did I know he'd be like the human men who'd broken my heart and made me lose my ability to trust? It wasn't fair of me to judge him by someone as awful as Ethan, when Griff had shown me nothing but what a decent, honest guy he was.

Then my mother's voice rang in my ears. *Boys will be boys, Caroline, and all men cheat. If you want to be happily married, you need to get used to looking the other way.*

Bile rose in the back of my throat as I remembered getting a scolding and not sympathy when I'd broken up with Ethan. I hadn't wanted to know any more about my mother's twisted idea of love, even though her words had shattered me and the image of my own family. One thing I'd learned though. I wanted nothing to do with looking the other way.

My feet rattled the steel stairs as I descended the last few, pausing at the bottom as Griff joined me. I couldn't help but smile at the gorgeous candy cane. Boys might be boys, but Griff was no boy.

"Hurry!"

Griff grabbed my hand and ran toward the brightly painted van with me in tow. The driver's glittery reindeer antlers bobbled as he hung from the window and waved for us to move faster. We slid onto the back bench seat next to Olivia while Carl hopped in the passenger's seat. My hoop skirt flew up when I sat, and I gave a little shriek as I pressed it down with both hands to keep from flashing the world.

"New performers, Dixie?"

Carl grinned at the driver in the velvet reindeer bodysuit. "We're just giving them a ride."

"Dixie?" I asked Carl.

"Dixie Normus." He craned his neck to wink at me. "Our reindeer driver is Ida."

"Ida Slapter at your service." He glanced at us in the rearview mirror, fluttering impossibly long, golden lashes.

"Let's hit it, Ida," Carl aka Dixie said, glancing nervously around. "We need to get Candy Cane out of here without being seen."

Ida floored it, and we were flattened to our seats as we sped down the alley. "Say no more, Sandy Claus."

CHAPTER 27

Griff

The van screeched to a halt in another alley, and Ida shot a look over his shoulder. "If anyone was tailing us, I'm pretty sure I lost them."

"Along with a hub cap or two." Dixie adjusted his jingling cap.

Ida poked out his bottom, cherry-red lip. "You said we needed to avoid being seen."

"In Miss Slapter's defense," Liv said as she uncoiled her hand from around my arm. "I'm pretty sure we were a blur as we shot through town. Where are we, by the way?"

"Behind The Queen Bee." Dixie opened the van door and hopped out, jingling all the way.

"And far from any paparazzi," Ida added, "although I wouldn't mind if photographers were obsessed with me."

The sexy reindeer eyed me in the rearview mirror before getting out of the van, but there was nothing predatory or judgmental in his gaze. Olivia wiggled her way out next, mumbling about how it wasn't as easy as it looked to be a tree.

When it was just the two of us in the vehicle, Caroline put her hand over mine. "Thank you. You didn't have to do this."

"I did if it means you won't get in trouble."

Caroline twisted to me, tipping back her odd hat so her face was visible. She held my gaze and put her hand to my cheek. "I don't think I deserve you."

Before I could tell her that she deserved everything, she brushed her lips across mine, sending jolts of pleasure down my spine and provoking a deep growl from my throat. Then she scooted across the seat and let Dixie help her from the van.

A hiss of air escaped from my gritted teeth as I followed her, swinging both legs from the vehicle since the column of spangly fabric was too snug to leap out like I normally would. Caroline and Olivia were already hurrying toward the door with Ida as I paused to adjust my outfit.

Dixie thumped me on the back as he slid the door shut behind me. "I hope you stick around for a while, Griff. Caroline deserves someone nice, and I know nice when I see it."

"She does not want me to stick around. She wants me to find someone else."

The white curls swung around Dixie's face as he shook his head. "With the way she looks at you? Not a chance. She might not know it yet, but the last thing she wants is you with someone else. Trust an old queen on this, doll."

"You are a queen?" I knew some parts of the Earth had royalty, but I had not thought New York was one of them.

Dixie threw back his head and laughed. "The only kind with any real panache, hon." He looped an arm through mine. "Now let's get you inside before you're spotted."

We hurried across the alley and through a dirty metal door that led to a dimly lit hallway with scuffed walls and a low ceiling. I couldn't see Caroline or Olivia or the spangly reindeer who'd driven us, but I could hear the rhythmic thump of music and the chatter of voices. The smell of trash and fuel from the alley gave way to the pungent aroma of food and perfume, both heavy and cloying.

"Word of advice from Sandy Claus?" Dixie said as he hustled me down the hallway. "Don't eat the clams."

From the amount of grime on the floors and dust gathering in the corners, I suspected avoiding any food would be a wise choice. "What is The Queen Bee?"

Dixie gave me a scandalized look. "Only the best drag nightclub in the city." Then a smile crossed his face, and he squeezed my arm. "But of course, you wouldn't know that since you're from out of town," he chuckled to himself, "way out of town."

My universal translator was fumbling over part of his explanation. "Drag?"

He waved a hand up and down his costume. "Adult dress-up for those of us with dramatic tendencies and a love of fashion."

I thought of the Cleverians and their habit of shifting genders and clothing accordingly. This didn't seem much different. "This is where you work?"

Another rumbling laugh from Dixie. "Only in the evenings. By day, I work in insurance, which is so boring it makes watching paint dry seem titillating." He elbowed me and smiled. "Then I come here and have some fun."

I was both intrigued and confused by humans. They were much more complex creatures than I'd thought they would be before I'd arrived, and the more of them I met, the less able I was to put them in neat categories. The females were especially confusing. I thought of Caroline telling me she couldn't be my mate and then kissing me, and my brain ached trying to figure out the truth beneath the confusion.

Dixie steered me past a thick-necked man in an emerald-green suit standing guard outside a room jammed with racks of clothes, mirrors on the walls, and more garishly-clad people with enormous hair and glittery outfits. Caroline and Olivia sat in worn, fabric chairs in the center of the room, while Ida assessed himself in one of the mirrors.

"You'll be safe here during the show." Dixie pulled me toward a vacant chair next to Caroline and dropped the paper shopping bag of our clothes at my feet. "No one knows you're here." He jerked his head toward the door and the man in the green suit. "And Jerry won't let anyone in he doesn't know."

Caroline took off her fringed hat. "I owe you one."

Dixie fluttered a hand at her. "Just tell me when all the good sales happen at Saks and we'll call it even, hon." Then Dixie flounced off to attend to the performers clustering around the mirrors and applying even more color to their eyelids.

A red light flashed over the door, prompting Ida to shout, "Showtime!"

Almost everyone rushed from the room in a flurry of excited whispers and nervous chatter, heels rapping on the hard floor and tall hairdos bobbling.

Caroline sank back in her chair when we were left alone in the room after the stampede. "What do we do now?"

Olivia stood and flung off her long, green ruffled dress to reveal her clothing beneath. "We blow this joint and start doing some serious image rehab on both of you."

CHAPTER 28

Caroline

*A*s I watched Liv efficiently distribute clothing from the paper shopping bag Dixie had left, I slumped into the chair. Image rehab? After the chaotic past few days, the last thing I wanted to do was any type of public relations. All I really wanted was to crawl into bed and eat cookies.

Cookies! I groaned as I remembered the unbaked sugar cookies we'd left sitting on sheet pans in my galley kitchen. What I wouldn't give to be nibbling on one now, instead of sitting in a tired dressing room with painted cinderblock walls that look like a Maybelline-sponsored tornado had ripped through it.

Liv handed me my yoga pants and tank top, which I eyed. They'd been perfect when I'd been in my well-heated apartment, but the basement dressing room was not so toasty. Suddenly, I was overcome with weariness. I was tired of my thankless job, I was tired of my demanding boss, and I was tired of pretending that the holidays weren't happening when the entire city was bursting with Christmas cheer.

Before I could scout out a place to change, my purse vibrated. I found my phone and flinched at the number on the screen. It was my mother, who I hadn't spoken to since she'd told me that I was the one in the wrong for breaking up with a guy who wasn't faithful.

I watched the phone buzz in my hand, fully prepared to let it go to voicemail. The last thing I needed was her judgment on the photos of me online. Then I remembered something. My mother didn't do social media.

She had a Facebook profile she never used; she didn't tweep—her words—and she probably didn't know of the existence of TikTok. There was no way she could have seen the images of me and Griff, which meant she was calling for another reason.

My pulse quickened at the possibility that she could be calling about the holidays. Maybe they wanted me to come home badly enough that she was willing to drop her constant barbs about me losing the best chance of happiness I'd ever have. Maybe someone was sick, or worse, dead.

Standing up, I answered the call as I walked outside the room. "Hey, Mom." I nodded to the burly guy guarding the door and took a few steps in the other direction.

"Caroline." She released an audible whoosh of breath. "I'm so glad you answered." I didn't respond so she let out a tight laugh. "You're always so busy these days. I leave messages, but…well, anyway…"

"How's Dad?" I asked. "Are you both okay?"

"Of course, we're okay. We still take our walks every morning, you know."

"That's good." At least this wasn't a call to tell me one of them was dying.

"Honey," my mother's voice softened, "why don't you come home for Christmas? It won't be the same without you here."

My gut twisted as her words arrowed straight through me. Being alone for Christmas wasn't what I wanted either, but I also knew I couldn't take another emotional onslaught like the one she'd pulled last year. Then the breakup had been fresher, but hearing her go on and on about what a great guy Ethan was and how he deserved my forgiveness had ruined the holidays for me and landed me at the airport early trying to catch any flight back to New York.

Liv had picked me up from Newark, which was the only airport I could fly into on short notice, and she'd consoled me the entire ride back. I did not want a repeat of that situation no matter how sad it would be to spend Christmas Day alone.

"I don't know, Mom. You know how busy the store gets at Christmas. We even book personal shopping appointments on Christmas Eve."

She huffed out an impatient breath. "They work you too hard. I don't know why you want to work for a big company in a big city when there are perfectly nice jobs down here." Her tone shifted again. "I don't want to argue with you, honey. I just wanted to tell you how much we want you to come home. It won't be the same without you opening presents with us on Christmas morning in our matching pajamas."

As cheesy as it was, I did love that we all got matching PJs on Christmas Eve and wore them that night and the next morning as we opened presents and sipped hot cocoa. Another pang of longing pulsed through me. Maybe I should go home. Surely my parents had gotten over me breaking up with the guy they'd hoped would be their son-in-law. It would be nice to eat my mother's famous pecan pie and sleep in my old bed.

"Honey, I'm worried about you. That soulless city isn't good for you."

I frowned. "The city is great. There's no place more festive than New York City at Christmas."

"But look what it's doing to you."

I hesitated, not sure what she was talking about. "What is it doing to me?"

Another tortured release of breath. "We're worried about you. Ethan is worried about you. We just want—"

"Ethan?" I cut off her sentence with a single, barked word. When she didn't speak, I shifted the phone from one shaky hand to the other, pressing it into the ear that wasn't hot. "When did you talk to Ethan?"

"Did you expect me to cut off all communication with him, Caroline? The boy was like family to us."

"Until I found out he was screwing a Pilates instructor during his lunch hour. Then he should have stopped being like family to you."

"Oh, Caroline." The disdain dripped from her voice. "You aren't still going on about that, are you?"

I fought the urge to scream as I gritted out a question. "When did you talk to Ethan?"

"If you must know, he called us earlier today and told us all about you being in compromising photos," she dropped her voice as if someone was listening to our conversation, "with an alien."

Blood pounded in my head as my entire body shook. She wasn't calling because she wanted me to come home for Christmas. She was calling because Ethan had gotten her upset about Griff. This was all about Ethan wanting something only when he thought he couldn't have it. My mother was still on Ethan's side, and the lying cheat knew it.

I bit back the sharp response I wanted to scream into the phone. It wouldn't do any good. In my mother's world, women looked the other way when their men strayed and welcomed them back with a warm hug and a cold beer. But that wasn't my world. I might not fully believe that I was as amazing as Griff seemed to think, but I knew I deserved better than this.

"Goodbye, Mom. Merry Christmas."

"What? You're not coming home?" Now she sounded desperate. "But I told Ethan—"

"You lied to Ethan? Then you two have a lot in common." I took a deep breath as she sucked in a shocked breath. "No, I can't come home for Christmas—this one or any other."

Then I disconnected amidst her spluttering and gasping, and I turned back to the dressing room and squared my shoulders. That had felt good.

CHAPTER 29

Griff

Olivia stared at the door Caroline had exited. "Well, that's not great."

I followed her gaze, not sure why Caroline answering her device could be bad.

"Nothing good ever comes from a phone call from her mother." Olivia shook her head as she pulled out her own device. "I wonder if she found out."

"Found out what?"

She glanced up, her gaze pointed. "Caroline's mother isn't the type of woman who'd be excited to see a picture of her daughter with a half-naked alien. I honestly don't know if it would be the half-naked part or the alien part that would bother her more."

"She does not approve of aliens? I thought Earth welcomed the Drexian reveal, and females were lining up to be brides."

The dark-haired woman lifted one shoulder. "Not everyone, but to be honest, I doubt Caroline's mother would be happy with anything she didn't control. And she thought she could control things with Caroline's ex." Olivia shuddered. "Good riddance to that douche."

I was unfamiliar with the word, but I didn't need to ask her for the definition to understand it was not flattering. "Does he have brown prickly hair?"

She tilted her head to one side. "Do you mean spiky? I guess it's spiky in the front." Her mouth gaped. "Why? She doesn't still have photos of him in her apartment, does she? I thought we burned them all during the mojo cleaning ritual."

I shook my head and tried not to think about the strange rituals of humans. "I think she saw him when I was on my date."

"At the ice rink?" She scraped a hand through her hair. "How did he know she was there?" Then she groaned. "Because of all the social media attention I drummed up. Nice going, Liv."

"She did not appear pleased to see him."

"I'll bet. They haven't spoken in a year."

I remembered seeing his hand holding her and the angry expression on his face. "He was not happy when she rejected him."

She rolled her eyes. "Typical. He comes from money, so he's used to sailing through life doing what he wants."

"I thought that Earth governments had laws so that each citizen was treated equally."

Olivia barked out a laugh. "Maybe in theory, but if you've got money, you get to play by different rules."

Earth was turning out to be very different than I'd expected. My ears caught snatches of Caroline's raised voice in the hallway. As her friend had predicted, it did not sound like her conversation was going well. I thought about the last conversation I'd had with my father, and I felt a pulse of sympathy for the human.

Olivia swiped on her screen. "Okay, it doesn't seem like the paps know where we are or that you and Caroline left her place. The only new photos are of her apartment window, which means they're still camped out front." She sat back down as she tapped on her device. "I'm not going to tell Miranda where we are, but I am going to tell her that I have everything under control." She glanced at me. "You should get changed, not that I don't love seeing you dressed like a sexy candy cane, but outside of a drag club, you're actually harder to hide in that getup."

I looked down at the clothing in my hands and at the striped dress that cocooned my body. I would not miss the itchy fabric or how hard it was to move in the narrow skirt. While Olivia tapped away on her device, I walked behind a rack of clothes, peeled off the dress, and quickly redressed in my black garments. I made my best attempt to hang the dress neatly on the rack before rejoining Caroline's friend.

When I took the chair across from her, she stole a quick glance at me and nodded her approval. "Much better."

Caroline walked back into the room, her shoes tapping on the floor and her jaw tight.

"Not good," Olivia mumbled so low only I could hear her, then gave Caroline a tentative smile. "How's your mom?"

"What do you think?" Caroline stopped and rapped one toe of her shoe rapidly. "I thought she might be calling to tell me how much they wanted me to come home for Christmas, which she did, but it was only because she'd talked to Ethan and was freaking out that I might be doing unspeakable things with…" Her jumble of words faded, and she made a point of not meeting my gaze. "I can't believe she's still taking his side over mine." Her voice wobbled. "I'm her daughter."

Olivia rushed to her and pulled her into a hug. "Forget about your parents and what they want. You don't need them or their screwed-up approval. You're doing great on your own."

"Thanks, Liv."

Olivia pulled back and squeezed the side of Caroline's shoulders. "That's not the only reason you're going to be thanking me. I've worked some PR magic and gotten another date lined up for Griff. Now the hashtag 'second date' is trending instead of the pictures of the two of you."

"I do not want a second date," I said.

"Not a second date with Beth," Olivia craned her head over her shoulder to meet my gaze. "I know she wasn't a love match for you. This is a new woman."

"I do not want a new woman."

Both females pivoted to stare at me, but Caroline's expression was less confused and more pleading.

I locked eyes with her. "I have already found who I want."

Olivia looked back and forth between us for a few moments before slapping a hand on her leg. "I knew it!"

Caroline shook her head even as her eyes became watery. "There's nothing to know. I told you that you can't pick me. I'm too much of a mess. You deserve someone who can actually love you. Not someone who's too terrified of getting hurt to even try."

"Caroline." Olivia's voice was soft as she stepped closer, but Caroline pulled away.

"You can't fix this, Liv. You can't fix me. I thought I was better. I thought I was over it, but I'm too broken." She blew out a shuddering breath. "Find him someone great, but it can't be me."

Then she turned on her heel and ran, and my heart twisted in my chest as if it had been beneath her foot.

CHAPTER 30

Caroline

$\mathcal{I}$ didn't look back as I fled the room, but I also didn't barrel down the painted cinder block hallway toward the alley. I ran toward the thumping music and raucous screams. It would be easy to disappear into the crowd at a drag show, especially since I still wore the gold lame dress that made me look like a lampshade. At least without the matching hat, I looked a bit less like a walking lamp.

Following the pounding beat of the music and the winding hall, I finally pushed open a heavy door, fought my way through thick velvety curtains that held the aroma of stale cigarette smoke, and stumbled into blinding lights. It took me a beat to realize I was on stage and the lights beating hot on me were stage lights. I swung my head to take in the performers sashaying across the wooden floor in a line. I must have literally walked into the big opening number. Before I could back away, a hand grabbed me and pulled me into the conga line.

"Smile and kick, sweetie."

I recognized Carl's gravelly voice and peered up at the white ringlet curls framing his face and the red Santa cap pinned to his wig. He gave me a bright smile and propelled me forward with him.

I squinted at the crowd, even though the light made it hard to see anything but faceless heads and waving arms. Still, I didn't want to let my neighbor down and ruin his show, so I plastered a smile on my face and mimicked his high kicks.

Once we'd crossed the stage and shifted to the back of the dancing group, he cut a quick glance at me. "What are you doing out here? I thought I told you to stay hidden in the back."

"I needed to leave," I said, while keeping my smile bright and facing the audience.

Mrs. Claus did jazz hands and shook his limited cleavage. "Where are the other two? Where's your alien?"

"He's not my alien." I heard the crack in my voice. "But he's why I needed to leave."

"Too bad," Carl said over the music, "he's the best one you've ever brought around."

When I gave him a questioning look, he worked a shrug into his dance moves. "What? I have eyes. I saw the one who used to come over but never took you out, and the one who thought he was God's gift to women and who would call other girls as soon as he left your place." Another shrug. "I also have ears, doll."

"Well, you're right. They were all jerks, but all of them ruined me for anyone else. I can't look at a guy without thinking of all the ways he could hurt me."

Carl hooked his arm through mine and spun me around like we were square dancing. "Not much of a way to go through life. You'll never find love if you don't drop those walls of yours."

I knew he was right, but I also remembered just how much it hurt to be betrayed and to realize that the person you'd trusted had humiliated you. While I'd been thinking about honeymoon spots, he'd been busy planning where to meet up with his side piece. That sick feeling slammed into me as fresh as it had been the day I'd discovered Miss Pilates wrapped around my boyfriend and learned what an idiot I'd been.

I shook my head and hoped it was in time to the music. "I can't. Griff deserves someone who isn't a hot mess like me."

Carl pulled me close with one hand and then flung me away in a spin. When he pulled me back in, he winked. "Welcome to the epicenter of hot messes. We're all a work in progress. Give yourself a break, hon."

I knew in my heart that everything Carl said was true, but I couldn't seem to let go of my fear. It had gripped me for so long that it was like a security blanket I couldn't relinquish. My fear had become my safe haven—a wall that protected me from feeling too deeply and being hurt again—even if it did get lonely.

"I can't. Not yet." I gave his hand a squeeze before I released it on the next spin and twirled my way to the edge of the stage and the stairs leading down. Without a backward glance, even though I could hear my name being called, I hurried from the stage and wound my way through the tables.

The patrons were cheering and clapping, so I did a few awkward dance moves and waved my own hands in the air. Money was shoved in my hands, so I shook my hips more and ruffled the hair off a few men. This got me even more cash, which I gratefully accepted, especially since I'd forgotten my purse.

I finally threaded my way to the back of the club. A doorman with silvered hair arched an eyebrow at me and gave me a thorough head-to-toe look.

"You're new."

"Carl brought me," I said as I straightened the crumpled cash in my hands.

He nodded as he opened the door for me. "You're good. I might even believe you're a real dame."

I smiled and thanked him. Considering the pool of single men in the city, I'd had worse compliments.

The frigid December air hit me the moment I stepped from the club, but I wrapped my bare arms around myself and hurried toward the curb, flagging down the first cab I spotted. I slid inside and across the leather back seat patched with duct tape, holding down the hoop skirt as it tried to fly forward.

"Where to?"

That stumped me. I couldn't return to my apartment since it was being staked out by paparazzi and TMZ wannabes. I could go to work, but then Miranda would pepper with me a thousand questions and want to know why I wasn't with my client. Olivia's place was out since she wasn't with me, and one of her three hundred snarky roommates would undoubtedly be home. Then I remembered The Plaza.

Griff had added my name to the room when we'd left in case I didn't get back into my apartment and needed to return before him. That was when Olivia had been convinced that his date would be a love match, and he'd be off with Beth for the rest of the day.

"The Plaza."

As the taxi jerked forward, I ripped the hem of the dress and pulled out the stiff hoop. I would owe Carl a new dress, but it was a small price to pay for not looking like a living lampshade.

CHAPTER 31

Griff

Olivia glanced from her phone as I stepped from the car driven by another Mr. Lyft. "I still have no idea where she went, and I can't figure out how she left the club so fast. We were in that alley right after she ran off, and there was no sign of her." She frowned and waved her screen at me. "Her phone is off, but I'll keep looking. Don't worry. We'll find her."

I wanted to tell the female not to worry. If Caroline was so convinced she could not be with me, I did not want to force her. I'd come to Earth to find a willing mate, not to strong-arm a human into accepting me. I didn't want to admit that my pride was hurt, since Valorians were taught to temper pride and the desire for personal glory, but watching Caroline run from me had hurt. I'd been sure that she was the one, but even a true mate could not be coerced into a match.

I craned my head to peer at the grand edifice of the hotel, with two tall green trees covered in twinkling lights flanking the entrance and large flags fluttering over the glass awning, before glancing back at the female in the car. "Thank you for your help, but I do not want you to chase down Caroline on my account."

Olivia's face fell. "What? Don't tell me you've changed your mind about her."

"I have not changed how I feel about your friend, but—"

Whew!" Olivia cut me off with a loud exhale. "As long as you're still into her, leave the rest to me."

It might have only been a short time, but I'd already learned not to argue with the energetic and strong-willed female. "Thank you for helping me and for looking for Caroline. You are a good friend."

Her expression became solemn. "She's an even better friend to me, and she deserves happiness more than you know." Then the grin returned to her face. "Which is why I'm going to fix this." She closed the car door and waved as it lurched away from the curb and back into traffic.

I did not think Caroline's decision was something that could be fixed, but I also knew I could not stop Olivia if I'd tried. I trudged up the red, carpeted stairs to the hotel and pushed my way through the odd spinning door as weariness washed over me.

The day had been long and chaotic, although most of it had not been unpleasant. After so long spent on space vessels, I'd enjoyed spending time outside and getting to see parts of the city I'd never imagined existed. I'd seen performers in a holiday show, although it had left me even more confused about Christmas, and I'd learned about Earth sweets called cookies.

My thoughts went to making cookies with Caroline and then quickly drifted to kissing her and ending up on her bed. Suddenly, my heart was racing as I remembered how soft she'd felt and how sweet she'd tasted.

I was so caught up in the swirl of memories that I barely noticed the towering tree in the entrance and the buzz of conversation that shifted as I walked past the front desk and into an empty elevator compartment. Despite my distraction, I was aware of the curious looks and whispered questions that I suspected were about me. Olivia had explained to me that I'd become famous—social media famous as she'd put it—and people would probably be filming me all the time in public.

I still did not understand this human concept of fame for fame's sake, and I found it odd that anyone would be interested in me without knowing who I was. Not that revealing my true identity would simplify matters.

The elevator dinged and the doors opened to my floor just as my device buzzed in my pocket. I retrieved it and scowled at the screen, even though I knew I could not ignore it.

I answered as I strode down the thickly carpeted hallway, bracing myself as the familiar face appeared on the screen. "Father."

His blue eyes glittered hard and sharp. "Your visit to Earth has not gone as planned."

I used the flat card to open the door to my suite, stepping inside as I answered. "According to your plan."

He scoffed at this and raked a hand through dark hair that matched mine. "My plan is the only one that matters. You are the Prince of Valoria, but you cannot ascend to the throne without a mate by your side."

I clenched my teeth. "I am aware of my duty."

"Are you? Do you know what will happen to our world if there is no leader?"

"You are leader."

His face contorted with pain for a beat. "I am dying."

My throat constricted to the point where I could not speak. I had always known my role and my duty, but the unspoken agreement was that my father would live to a very old age before I needed to take his place. After losing my mother when I was young, my father's solid presence had been the one constant in my life, even as I'd traversed the galaxy in my duties as a Valorian warrior. Knowing that he was ruling on our home world as I fought to defend it had always made my absence from Valoria bearable. But now...

"We do not know that," I said, when I'd found my voice.

"We do," he snapped back. "My time is growing short, and your time to rule is fast approaching." His voice softened. "You must find a mate and be bonded to her in the ancient ritual before I am gone."

"I am trying. It is not so simple—"

"This is about the survival of your world and your species. There are enemies who would love to exploit the weakness of a planet without a lawful ruler." His face twisted again, and he hissed out a pained breath. "You did not want any of the remaining Valorian females, which I understood. I gave you leave to find a human mate since the Drexians have had luck with the species, but there is no more time to waste. Find a female—any female who can bear you offspring—and take her as your mate before you send our planet into chaos."

The agony in his words and face was evident, and pain knifed through my own heart as it did each time I saw the father I'd idolized wither away more and more with each passing day. I despised myself for staying away from him so I wouldn't see him fade, so I wouldn't be forced to acknowledge my loss, and I knew I owed him this much.

I squared my shoulders and gave him a curt nod. "I will, Father. You have my word."

He smiled at me then, although it was weary. "You have always made me proud, son. I know you will be a great king."

Then his image vanished, and I walked woodenly to the nearest chair and collapsed into it, the weight of being the next ruler of my people crushing me with each step. I braced my elbows on my knees and put my head in my hands. Then I heard a rustling from the next room and jerked toward the sound.

Caroline stood in the doorway to the bedroom. "You're a prince?"

CHAPTER 32

Caroline

I hadn't meant to listen to Griff's conversation, but when he'd walked into the suite, I'd been too startled to do anything but run into the bedroom. I should have announced my presence when I realized he was on a personal call with his father, but then his father had called him a prince, and all rational thoughts had fled my brain.

I'd stood stock-still in the bedroom as I'd learned that not only was Griff a prince of his planet and the future ruler, but that he was going to ascend to the throne soon. My heart had lurched when his father had said he was dying, but that sympathy was soon forgotten when I'd heard his father remind him that he had to find a bride fast, or he would not be able to become king. I didn't understand the way Valorian society worked, but it sounded like the stability of the entire species depended on Griff finding a mate, like, yesterday.

Information that would have been helpful before he hired me to find him a bride, I thought, or before I let myself fall for him.

I couldn't believe he hadn't mentioned any of this when he'd employed me to be his personal shopper for the perfect wife, but what really made my pulse spike was that he hadn't brought it up when we'd been alone. There had been plenty of chances for him to reveal the truth of his trip to Earth, but especially before he'd practically charmed me out of my pants in my apartment. I'd been in serious danger of falling for him, but all the while he was just looking for the woman who'd be the fastest route to inheriting his crown.

A sick feeling washed over me. Had he pegged me as the easiest woman to woo? Did I have sucker written across my forehead? Ethan had clearly sensed that I'd be easy to trick and manipulate, but had Griff done the same thing?

I shook my head as he made his final vows to his father. I didn't want to believe that the alien had been tricking me the entire time, but how else could I explain such huge omissions? He hadn't wanted to tell me why his need to find a bride was urgent because what woman would want to agree to marry a guy just because he was desperate?

Probably plenty, I thought, especially once they discovered that Griff was an alien prince and soon-to-be king. The alien-chasers would probably claw out each other's eyes to become the next queen of Valoria.

Well, not me. I was done being lied to and manipulated. It didn't matter that I'd felt things for Griff that I hadn't felt for anyone else—not even Ethan, and I'd thought I was going to marry him one day—or that I hadn't felt as comfortable with any guy as I had with the Valorian. I pushed aside the memories of his hands roaming my body and sending frissons of heat buzzing across my skin. I didn't want to think about how his kisses had made my head swim and heat pool restlessly in my core. None of that changed the fact that he hadn't told me the truth, and I couldn't bear being deceived again. Not even if my gut told me that Griff was nothing like my ex-boyfriend.

I stepped into the doorway and spotted Griff sitting on one of the upholstered chairs with his head in his hands. He looked completely defeated, and some of my anger seeped away. Then he looked up, his eyes wide as they met mine. For a moment, I forgot everything as his intense, blue gaze locked on mine. Then I remembered what I'd heard, and why I'd been so upset.

"You're a prince?"

He blinked at me like he was seeing a mirage. "Where did you come from?"

I tried to ignore the fact that I'd basically crashed his hotel room, even though it didn't look good for me to appear from the bedroom like I'd been lying in wait while he was on a private call with his father. "I didn't have my purse and I couldn't go back to my apartment, so I came here." When he looked at me blankly, I added. "You put my name on the room, remember?"

He glanced at the device in his hands, as if it had just hit him what I'd heard.

"You should have told me that you're a prince," I tried to regain some of my righteous indignation, although it was hard with the guy looking so defeated.

"It was not relevant information."

I gaped at him, outrage stirring fresh within me. "Not relevant? You asked me to help you find a mate for life without mentioning that you're about to inherit a kingdom. That's pretty crucial information."

"Why? I do not wish to attract females who are only interested in my title."

He had a point there. The alien-chasers would lose their damn minds once they discovered that this guy was alien royalty. "That doesn't change the fact that you should have told *me*." My throat tightened. "Or did you think I would treat you differently?"

He studied me for a moment. "You would not, but you are not interested in being mine."

Now my throat practically closed on me. I'd definitely told him that I couldn't be with him, but to say I wasn't interested wasn't exactly true. Not that he'd been truthful with me. "You lied about why you needed a bride. You should have told me why you were here, and why it was so important to find the right person quickly."

"I never lied to you." He stood, the dejected look fading from his face. "I do not lie."

I released an aggravated sigh. Even though Griff hadn't lied, his secrets made me feel like I'd been fooled again. All the old feelings of betrayal rushed to the surface, and my heart raced as I tried not to remember how awful it had been to discover that I'd been cheated on and lied to for months. "But you withheld information. It's the same thing."

"You wished me to tell you everything, even though I did not know you?" His blue eyes blazed with intensity. "I did not require that you reveal all your pain to me."

My mouth fell open. What did he know of my pain? Had he heard my conversation with my mother? I shook off his comment, even though the truth of it rang in my ears. "You're right. I didn't tell you everything about me because I barely know you, which is probably why you didn't trust me enough to tell me why you came to Earth. I guess the truth is neither of us know each other."

Griff opened his mouth, but I didn't wait for him to explain. I was too scared that he would make it all sound harmless, and I would accept his explanations, just like I'd done for months with Ethan when he'd convinced me that I'd been imagining things. Despite knowing in my heart that Griff was different, I couldn't fall for anyone's deception ever again.

"You might not have owed me the truth, but now that I know, I'm not sure if I can trust you. I don't even know the real you."

I barreled toward the door and yanked it open.

"I have always been myself with you, even if you did not know my title."

My gut clenched at his words. As I looked back at Griff, I knew one thing above all else. I couldn't trust myself with him. "Goodbye, Prince Griff."

CHAPTER 33

Griff

I stood in the bedroom of the hotel suite with a black travel bag open on the rumpled covers of the bed that betrayed my tortured sleep. Sunlight streamed through the windows, assaulting my eyes, and my head ached.

My conversation with my father had had the opposite effect that the ailing Valorian had intended, and Caroline leaving had added to my sense of despair. Maybe I should have gone after her, but a part of me knew she'd been right.

I hadn't lied, but I hadn't told her the truth, either. Not that I would have unloaded my planet's precarious situation to the first human I encountered, but as we'd grown closer, I could have told her. But telling anyone would have been admitting out loud that my father was dying. A part of me was able to move forward and prepare to assume the duties of my position, but only if I could put all the attending pain in a separate part of my brain.

If I thought about my father's death and being left completely without family, my gut churned, my head pounded, and I was taken right back to being a small Valorian after my mother died. The planet mourned the loss of their queen, while I quietly wept over the idea that she would never hold me again or comfort me when I was convinced I could not meet my father's impossibly high standards for me at the royal academy.

Even though I felt more at home with Caroline than I had with anyone in a very long time, I could not tell her that I needed a bride because I could not assume the crown without one. That would be admitting that the Valorian crown was being foisted upon me before I wished it because my father was dying. Telling her any of it would make it real, and the only way I could survive was by ignoring the pain that threatened to crush me.

I crossed to the wardrobe and pulled a garment from a hanger, folding it once before dropping it in my bag. My father would be disappointed if I left Earth without a mate, but I could not continue to search for one when my heart was already taken. I didn't know how I'd managed to fall for the one single female in the city who seemed to consider herself unavailable, but Caroline now occupied my thoughts to the point where I couldn't even think of another.

"Foolish," I muttered to myself.

I'd come to Earth with a list and an agenda. It was supposed to be a straightforward task. Find a female who checked off all the boxes and make her my mate. Return to Valoria with my new bride, ready to ascend to the throne when…

I gave my head a hard shake. I couldn't think of being king without grief washing over me, and the only reason I was rushing to find a mate was because of my lineage and duty to the crown. It was no way to choose a mate or start a life together.

Caroline's amusing chaos had made it easy for me to forget about the reason for coming to Earth. Between helping her when she'd lost her keys and then teaming up to escape the notice of the paparazzi by dressing in bizarre costumes, I'd been so busy adapting to the city and the general calamity to let my reality intrude. As strange as most of it had been, I'd been able to be myself without her knowing my true identity or my sad truth.

Truth.

The word made me flinch. Caroline had accused me of being untruthful. I had never lied to her, but I had been holding back a big part of myself. If she'd just been my personal shopper, that would have been understandable. But she had become more to me, and it was impossible to deny that I'd wanted her to be mine. Had I truly thought she could accept me with so much untold between us?

It had been foolish of me to think that any female could agree to become my mate without knowing all of me. That is, any female worth having.

A hard knock on the door snapped me from my descent into self-pity, and I strode to the sound with hope fluttering in my chest. I threw it open, expecting to see Caroline. Instead, a tall Drexian with dark hair and scruff darkening his cheeks took long steps past me and into my suite. I turned and followed him, baffled by the appearance of the stranger.

When he reached the sitting area, he turned and crossed his arms over the decorated sash of his dark uniform. "I am High Commander Dorn of the Drexian Empire."

The name tickled a memory in the recesses of my brain, but it didn't resurface before I was shaking my head. What was a member of the High Command doing on Earth? An even better question was why was he in my hotel room?

"You are Prince Griff of the Valorians, son of King Armis."

"Did my father send you?"

Dorn shook his head and relaxed his stance. "I am aware of your mission here on Earth, but I was not sent by your father." He rasped a hand down the stubble on his cheeks. "I was sent by my wife."

"Your wife?" The words burst from my mouth before I could stop them or temper the shock in the tone.

Instead of being angry, Dorn chuckled. "I can understand your surprise. You do not know human females as well as I do."

"I do not know them well at all," I admitted, "or understand them."

Dorn sank onto the couch and leaned his forearms on his legs. "You have only been here a few days. Understanding human females is the work of a thousand lifetimes." When he saw the look on my face, he erupted with another laugh. "That's why I'm here. Our tribute bride program has been monitoring your search for a mate, and I've come with some advice."

Although I had traveled to the planet on a Drexian transport and with Drexians involved with the mate-matching program, it hadn't occurred to me that they would be monitoring my actions. I suppose I'd been naïve.

"I do not need your tips on finding a human mate." I took the seat across from High Commander Dorn. "I have terminated my search and will be leaving Earth."

"I know. We received your request for transport." His brow wrinkled. "I understand that your experience in the search for a mate has not been smooth, but that is no reason to abandon it. Like I said, it takes some time to understand the human females."

Frustration bubbled inside me. "Time is the last thing I have. I came here in need of a mate, but I have failed. I cannot waste any more time on a pointless mission."

Silence hung between us.

The Drexian cocked his head. "I know of your people. You are valiant warriors. You do not abandon a quest so quickly. Why give up on this one?"

I took a deep breath and fought to control my impatience with myself. "The females I do not want would be willing to run away with me without a second thought, but the one I desire…"

Dorn nodded and released a deep sigh. "I understand a few things about reluctant brides. Do you believe her to share your feelings?"

I thought back to Caroline being beneath me on her bed and the hunger hot in her gaze. "Yes, but she says she cannot give me what I want."

Dorn's bright-green eyes held mine. "What do you want?"

That was a question I'd been rarely asked. I was accustomed to being told my duty, not being asked my wishes. What did I want more than anything else? "I only want to be with her."

Dorn leaned back on the cushions with a self-satisfied grunt. "Then you do not give up on her."

I straightened, his confidence reminding me that I was a Valorian prince, and I did not give up, especially on someone I realized I could not bear to be without.

The Drexian cleared his throat. "I do have some hard-won tips on how to win a human's heart without being killed in the process."

CHAPTER 34

Caroline

"*T*his is a surprise."

I bristled at the sharp voice as heels clicked on the stairs from below. I'd only been back at my desk at The Fifth Avenue Club for a few minutes, but it had been wishful thinking to hope that my boss wouldn't sense my presence and pounce on the chance to berate me. Despite my professional black suit and tidy bun, I felt like I was still reeling from the past two days. Any appearance of composure was entirely manufactured.

"Hi, Miranda." I managed a smile while I stood and greeted the woman who stalked toward me like a ravenous predator.

She actually licked her lips, no doubt excited by the idea of ripping into me. "I'm surprised to see you here."

I didn't rise to the bait. I wouldn't be surprised if she fired me. Part of me wished that she would.

"Don't you have better things to be doing?" Miranda smiled slyly. "Or should I say, aliens to be doing?"

I steadied my breath and returned her smile. "I'm not involved with the Valorian. I'm sorry our attempts to match him weren't successful, but the images you saw misrepresented the work Olivia and I did on his behalf."

"Work that failed to get our client what he wanted."

I shifted from one foot to the other. "So far."

Her dark brows popped high. "So far? You're still working with him?"

It would be a lie to say that I was still working with Griff, but he'd never formally terminated our working relationship. "Let's just say that finding the perfect bride for an alien isn't something that happens overnight."

She eyed me up and down. "Then why are you here now?"

Good question. Why was I there instead of curled up in bed licking my wounds and reveling in my cowardice? Maybe because I'd tossed and turned all night and couldn't bear to stay in my apartment a moment longer. Not when it reminded me of cutting out cookies with Griff, and then doing much less Christmassy activities on my bed. Even seeing my neighbor's door brought back memories of Griff dressed like a drag queen named Candy Cane.

The truth was that I'd been hoping that my usual parade of demanding clients would distract me from thinking of Griff's face when I'd stormed from his hotel room. Every time I thought about how sad he'd looked after talking to his father, and then how angry I'd been at him, a sick feeling roiled in my gut. All I needed was a few high-maintenance demands to purge the guilt from me, although I was afraid I'd never forget the empty ache of walking away from him.

"I hated the idea of you covering for me and Olivia while we were busy with the Valorian." I attempted to make my voice sound sincere as my boss narrowed her eyes at me. "I'm back to take some work off your plate."

Miranda raised a hand so she could drum her long fingers along her jaw. "That's sweet of you but completely unnecessary." She smiled like the cat that had caught the canary. "I've already replaced you."

My voice caught in my throat. "Replaced me?"

She pressed her lips together and nodded. "You might be cute enough to charm some alien out of his clothes, but pretty girls like you are a dime a dozen in this town."

As much as I'd dreaded the holiday rush of impossible wish lists, I needed this job. "That's not fair. I'm good at my job. My clients love me."

Miranda shrugged. "And they'll love the next blonde. Of course, I'm hoping your replacement can manage not to be an embarrassment and scandal magnet for the department." Her smile looked like bared teeth. "I warned you about fraternizing with the clients."

Tears stung the back of my eyelids. It was one thing to lose your job. It was another for your boss to basically accuse you of sleeping with a client.

Miranda stepped closer as if she was moving in for the kill. "Too bad you weren't even good at that. Next time you seduce a client, try not to scare them away."

"She did not seduce me or scare me away."

I whirled around just as quickly as my boss, but she recovered quicker than I did.

"What a pleasure to see you again in The Fifth Avenue Club." Miranda's voice had lost its hard edge and now poured from her poisonous lips like molasses.

"You are wrong about Caroline," Griff glared at Miranda, his voice thunderous. "She is not an embarrassment."

Miranda took a step back as Griff strode forward, his fiery gaze sliding from her to me. "She is kind, generous, funny, and tall."

I hitched in a ragged breath, shocked by his appearance at the store and by his defense of me. I'd given him no reason to want to see me again.

"Tall?" I managed to say.

Griff pulled out a device and held the screen out to me. "I have finished my list."

It took me a moment to realize what he meant. "You finished the list of qualities you want in a wife?"

"I made a list of all the things I admire about you and that is my new list." He glanced down at it. "Strong, stubborn, clever, accepting, draws beautiful pictures, and tastes like hot chocolate."

"Those are all things you like about me?" I'd never had anyone list things they liked about me or probably even think about something like that.

He peered up at me. "There are more."

"But I wasn't nice to you last night." I bit my lower lip. "I was scared, and I lashed out at you."

He met my gaze and shrugged. "I did not put that on the list."

"I guess I should make a list of all the great things about you and put forgiving at the top."

"There is nothing to forgive. I should have told you that I am the Prince of Valoria."

Miranda sucked in a breath, reminding me that she was there.

I shook my head. "I get why you didn't. You wanted to find someone who liked you for you. I wasn't mad at you, even though I thought I was. I was mad at someone from my past who has no business taking up any more space in my brain."

"I am not your puny human boyfriend."

I laughed at his assessment of Ethan. "No, you're definitely not." Then my smile dropped. "Can you forgive me for running because of the awful things he did, and not staying because of all the kind things you did?"

"Only if you will do me to the honor of marrying me."

My heart seized, making my voice come out like a strangled gasp. "What?"

"What?" Miranda shrieked.

"You want me?" My pulse raced and my hands trembled as he took them in his. "After everything that happened?"

He curled one arm around the small of my back. "Everything that happened is why I want you. From the moment you banged your head on that desk and agreed to help me, I knew that I'd found the one. I want to wake up next to you, and not sleeping on the floor in the next room. I want to hold your hand every day even if I am not trying to keep from losing you in a crowd. I want your art to decorate our palace, and I want our children to have your beautiful green eyes."

My eyes swam with happy tears as I sank into his embrace. "Since you put it like that, yes, I'll marry you."

He crushed his mouth to mine, his kiss sending shockwaves to the tips of my toes. When he tore his lips from mine, I smiled up in a daze. "You know what this means, don't you?"

"That you will be Queen of Valoria?"

I cast a glance over my shoulder at my boss who stared at us, slack-jawed. "It means I quit."

Griff also looked at her. "And I would like to terminate my relationship with your store. I'm afraid I do not like how you treat your staff."

"You know where we should go?" I grabbed his hand and pulled him with me away from the The Fifth Avenue Club. "Bloomingdale's."

Miranda emitted a pained scream, but neither of us looked back.

Griff squeezed my hand. "I do require many presents before we return to Valoria."

CHAPTER 35

Griff

"*I* thought you agreed to go to Bloomingdale's." Caroline gave me her best attempt at a severe look as I pushed open the door to my hotel suite, but her quivering lips betrayed her amusement.

"I will go to this Blooming-gales with you, but first…" I kicked the door closed behind her as I swung her into my arms.

She let out a laughter-filled shriek as I walked with her into the bedroom. "What are you—?"

I dropped her on the bed, and she bounced on her back. "I am resuming at the exact point where we were interrupted."

Caroline's pupils flared, and her laughter faded, as she sat up part way and started to tug at my shirt. "Then you can't have this. You weren't wearing a shirt when you were on my bed."

I growled as her fingers brushed my skin and sent scorching heat skittering across it. Gritting my teeth to keep some semblance of self-control, I helped her by yanking the garment over my head and tossing it aside.

She sucked in a breath as her gaze locked on my stomach muscles, and she ran her fingertips down the corded flesh, her nails scraping and leaving trails of pale blue behind. "You're so perfect."

I choked back a laugh as I stared down at her and threaded my fingers through her golden hair. "I can never be as perfect or as beautiful as you."

She tipped her head back, smiling at me. "From any other guy, that would sound like a line, but not from you."

I slid my hand from her hair to cup her chin in my palm. "It is the truth. I will never lie to you, and I will never withhold any information from you again."

She released a shuddering breath, and her smile widened. "I believe you." Then she circled her hands around my back and yanked me to her, pulling my mouth to hers in a hard kiss.

My knees went weak as I fell forward, bracing my body over hers on the bed as I quickly shifted the kiss so that my tongue was parting her lips and delving into her mouth. She moaned as my kiss became deep and claiming, and she wove her fingers into my hair and held me to her, even hitching her skirt up high and hooking her legs around my waist.

My entire body pulsed with pounding desire as I ground my cock into her, and her hands moved from my hair to my shoulders, and then to my back, where she scored my flesh as she arched into me.

With a quick move and without breaking our kiss, I flipped over so that I was on my back, and she was on top of me. Caroline emitted a surprised noise but then sank into me as I gripped her hips and rocked her body into mine.

I dragged my hands from her hips up her body, pulling at the blouse tucked into her skirt so I could get at the soft skin beneath. Caroline tore her lips from mine and leaned back, her gaze locking onto me as she shed her black suit jacket, then slowly unbuttoned her top and shrugged it from her shoulders.

I was riveted by her languid motions as she skimmed her long fingers across the soft mounds of her breasts and the white lace of her bra. She teased her fingertips across the hard peaks, which were hard under the thin fabric, and then flicked her fingers at a clasp in the center. The bra popped open, and her breasts spilled out, pebbled beige flesh tipping them.

I knifed up and set my mouth upon one and then the other, desperate to taste all of her. I sucked the bumpy peaks, swirling my tongue around them until her moans were loud and needy. Caroline's hands were braced on my shoulders, as she arched her back and let her head fall back and her hair spill down.

Suddenly, she straightened and ran her hands down my chest. "I thought you'd never been with a human female before."

"I haven't." I dragged my gaze from her luscious curves to meet her eyes. "But I was given some advice by the Drexians before I arrived."

She hummed, her lips curving into a smile. "That explains it."

Her hands continued moving down and when she reached the waistband of my pants, she scooted back a bit and fumbled for a moment before unfastening them. With a satisfied sigh, she released my cock, which sprang up, hard and long.

Caroline licked her lips as she ran one hand down the length of it, the rigid flesh so dark blue it was almost purple. Her fingertips caressed the firm ridge that encircled the base and curved up to a form a knob at the top, which was humming as it vibrated.

She glanced at me with a look of wonder on her face, then she bit the corner of her bottom lip. I slid one finger beneath the hitched-up fabric of her skirt and nudged aside the lace of her panties, growling when I felt how damp they were. "You are ready for me."

I slipped my finger through her slickness, finding the firm nub that I'd heard the Drexians talk about with reverence.

She gasped, her eyelids fluttering. "You got good advice."

I circled the slick bundle of nerves with my fingertip, watching her eyelids flicker as she opened her legs wider and leaned back, never releasing her grip on me. Swirling faster, I watched her breathing become ragged and her breasts quiver as she rocked into my hand.

I palmed one of Caroline's breasts, thumbing the nipple as I continued to work my finger over her pleasure center. Her keening noises sent heat straight to my cock, but there was nothing I wanted more than to hear her sounds of pleasure and feel her body shatter.

With a gasp, she arched her back and screamed as tremors wracked her body. Her grip on my cock tightened as she trembled and moaned, the skin in her chest flushing pink.

Before she'd caught her breath, Caroline gave me a hard push. I fell back as she angled herself over me, tugging aside her soaked panties and giving me a wicked grin. Then she was taking me inside, her tight heat enveloping my cock as she sat fully on me.

Her eyes went wide as her body rested on the raised rim at the base and my knob brushed her swollen flesh.

A raw, primal sound escaped from my clenched teeth as I fought not to explode from the pure pleasure humming through my body. "You are unlike anything I have ever experienced."

"Right back at you." Caroline braced her hands on my chest muscles, dragging in a breath as her body adjusted and her lips quirked. "I heard aliens were big, but I didn't know just how big. Now I understand why you were worried about finding a women who could take you."

I grabbed the side of her hips, fighting the desire to drive her up and down. "If I am too much—"

"You are, but in the best way." She twitched her hips, angling forward as my cock and knob buzzed and releasing a throaty moan. "I didn't know you vibrated."

I moved my hands, savoring the feel of her bare skin and trying to distract myself from the way her tight heat was gripping my cock. "Surprise."

She smiled wickedly as she started to move up and down, and then I gripped her hips tighter and took over. Caroline lifted her hands over her head, raking them through her hair as I slid her up and down. The sight of her giving herself over and letting me set the rhythm sent my heart into free fall and made my vibrations so powerful I could feel them through my hands.

My breath was hard and fierce and mingled with her soft, keening sounds that made it impossible for me to go slow. I clenched my jaw as I drove her down on me again and again, my desperate growls tangling with her cries until she fell forward and her body clenched around my cock, spasming so hard that I could hold back no longer. I exploded with a roar as I thrust up hard and held her on my cock, black spots dancing behind my eyelids as the planet seemed to jolt on its axis.

Caroline collapsed onto my chest, hitching in breaths that were as erratic as mine. I wondered if I could exist forever in that perfect moment with only the sounds of our breathing and the thudding of our hearts beating in sync. When she finally lifted her head to meet my gaze, her eyes were half-lidded. "That was officially the best surprise I've ever gotten."

EPILOGUE

Caroline

"These aren't half bad," I nibbled the edge of a sugar cookie as Griff and I stood in my galley kitchen, "especially since they sat out for so long without being baked."

Griff mumbled something as he shoved another cookie into his mouth.

I laughed and shook my head. "I guess you think they're pretty good."

He swallowed and eyed the rest of the cookies. "We do not have anything so good on Valoria. You will have to teach my people how to make coopies."

"Cookies," I corrected. "And I would be happy to bring an unhealthy love of baked goods to Valoria."

Griff curled his arms around me from behind and nuzzled my neck. "There is nothing bad about any part of your love."

Heat prickled my bare flesh, but I twirled from his grasp and wagged a finger at him. "Oh no, you don't. We agreed today was about, well, something else."

After spending an entire day in bed at the Plaza, I'd convinced him to return to my apartment so I could start packing—and so my body could recover from so much intense sex. I did want to be able to walk once I was on his home world.

"You're right." He looked slightly abashed. "Today is your Christmas."

In all the craziness of the past few days, I'd almost forgotten that it was the 25th of December. A small ache welled in my chest, but I pushed it aside. If I'd learned anything from the unpleasant scrutiny of the press, it was who my real friends were and who had my back. I was sad that my parents couldn't support me like I needed them to, but I had found people—and an alien—who did. Sometimes it was the friends you chose who became the family you needed.

A knock on the door almost made me drop the last bite of my cookie, but I popped it into my mouth as I walked from the galley kitchen and squinted through the peephole. My shoulders relaxed when I saw who was on the other side.

"What happened to the Mrs. Claus costume?" I asked Carl when I opened the door.

My neighbor no longer wore the wig of white ringlets and the red dress edged with fur. Instead, he was in a sequined green jumpsuit with a gold pointed collar.

"Sandy Claus is a lot to maintain on a daily basis." He winked at me. "I wanted to be a bit more casual for Christmas with friends."

He eyed my yoga pants and oversized red sweater. "You did get my message, didn't you?"

"Message?" My cheeks warmed. Had I checked my phone since I'd left Saks? I'd been so caught up in spending time with Griff that I had shut out the rest of the world.

Griff appeared behind me and circled an arm around my waist, which provoked a knowing smile from Carl.

"No explanations needed, darlings. I left you a message inviting you to Christmas dinner at my place, with some of the queens you met at the club." He flicked a hand toward his open door where drag queens were flouncing around a long table that stretched almost the entire length of the efficiency apartment.

Before I could respond, Liv appeared at the top of the stairs. Her cheeks were flushed, snow speckled her dark hair, and she held two red-and-green gift bags tall enough to hold wine bottles. "My kingdom for an elevator." When she saw us all, she beamed. "Oh, good. These two came up for air."

I tried to give her a look, but she was ignoring me as she rushed forward and thrust the bags at Carl. "I brought wine. It's cheap but sweet."

Carl cocked an eyebrow at her. "Just like me, hon." Then he spun on his heel and returned to his apartment, leaving the door standing open.

Liv slid her gaze to me and Griff, grinning like the Cheshire Cat. "I heard what you said to Miranda."

"You did? I didn't think she'd want to repeat that to anyone."

Liv nodded. "One of the new employees was within earshot and heard everything, and then she shared the gossip in the employee lounge. Miranda found out and fired her, so the woman made a

TikTok about the whole mess." She rubbed her hands together. "It went viral, and then Miranda got fired for losing such a famous client."

My jaw dropped. "I had no idea."

Olivia gave me a long up and down. "I'm sure you didn't." Then her face broke into a smile, and she threw her arms around me. "I'm so happy for you. I knew you and Griff made a great couple, but it took you long enough to figure it out."

When she pulled back, I glanced back at Griff. "We're engaged."

She put her hands to her cheeks. "This is so exciting. I can't wait to get started on wedding planning with you." She held up her hands, palms out in a stop-right-now gesture. "But first, it's Christmas Day, and I'm dying for some mashed potatoes and stuffing."

Now that she mentioned it, I wouldn't mind eating food other than cookies. The three of us walked into Carl's apartment and were met with the savory scent of roast turkey and cinnamon. I inhaled the intoxicating aroma as my stomach growled.

The long table was draped in a collection of cloths that resembled remnant pieces from fabric bolts, the various patterns and colors overlapping to cover the entire length. Mismatched plates ran from one end to the other along with glassware ranging from cut glass water glasses, to chunky goblets, to colored wine flutes. Dishes crowded the middle with aluminum foil covering the contents, even though steam snuck from the edges and curled into the air. Holiday music played in the background, but the warbly sound of Ethel Merman singing about Christmas in July was muffled by the chatter of the other guests.

"There they are!" The driver we knew as Ida Slapter ran up and gave us all quick hugs, but it took me a moment to place her without her antlers and reindeer bodysuit. Today, she wore a slinky red cocktail dress, although her eyeshadow was just as bright blue as it had been when she'd been on stage. "I'm so glad you three could make it."

"Who are these tasty treats?" A towering queen in the same red-and-white striped dress Griff had worn sauntered up to us, his blond beehive almost brushing the ceiling.

Ida rolled her eyes. "This is Rhoda."

"Rhoda Dendron," the queen clarified, giving us all appraising looks.

"Why don't we all sit down?" Carl announced from the other end of the table, waving us to three spots together.

I sat with Liv and Griff on either side of me while Ida elbowed Rhoda Dendron aside to sit next to Griff on his left. Bottles of wine were passed down the table, and we filled our own glasses as foil was removed from dishes and steam billowed from mounds of mashed potatoes, bowls of green beans, corn swimming in butter, a ham dripping with glaze, and a golden-brown turkey surrounded by stuffing. Baskets of warm rolls were passed around, the yeasty smell tickling my nose, while Carl carved the turkey with aplomb.

I took a sip of wine as everyone served themselves and chatted happily, glancing at Griff who was studying his device intently. I was all too aware that Griff had informed his father about me and his decision and had been waiting for his father's response. "Everything okay?"

He looked up at me, smiling. "Better than okay. My father was so pleased that I have found someone who makes me happy that his own condition had improved."

I put my hand over his and squeezed. "I told you Christmas was magical."

He nodded. "I am still not sure if I believe in your concept of magic, but I will agree that Christmas is unique and has a certain curious effect."

I glanced around the table of drag queens who were laughing and sharing food. "I don't know how, but it brings people together and makes the world a little bit brighter."

Griff nodded thoughtfully. "All the news from Valoria is not good, though."

I paused and swallowed my mouthful of sweet wine. "No?"

"My cousin, Ruune, heard about my journey to Earth and my success in finding you. Now he is convinced he should do the same."

"That's bad?"

Griff frowned. "Ruune has always been wild. I fear he does not want a mate as much as an excuse to bed many human females."

Liv leaned across me. "What was that? Did I hear that another Valorian might come here looking for a mate? I did do a pretty good job getting you two together."

I eyed her. "You put Griff on half a dozen dating apps."

"That was at the beginning." She waved away my comment. "I've learned more about Valorians since then."

"Why don't you focus on your maid of honor duties for now?"

Liv's mouth fell open. "You want me to be your maid of honor? Truly?"

I nodded as her eyes teared. "Of course. You don't expect me to plan a wedding on an alien world alone, do you?"

Olivia wrapped her arms around me and squeezed. "I'm so happy I'm not even going to think about how much I'm going to miss you."

"Oh, did I mention that Griff is a prince and will inherit the throne of Valoria?"

"You're going to be a queen?"

Liv's shrieked question made the entire table freeze. Then Carl raised a glass. "Join the club, sweetie."

I laughed as everyone clinked glasses, and Griff pulled me to him for a warm squeeze. *This* was my new favorite Christmas memory. I was with the guy I adored, surrounded by people who accepted me, with nothing but happy possibilities in my future.

I glanced out the window at the far end of the apartment to see snow swirling through the air, the flurries thick and fat. Not only was the dinner perfect and my husband-to-be a gorgeous prince, we'd gotten a white Christmas after all.

No matter what Griff thought, I knew the truth. Christmas was magical.

* * *

THANK you for reading CHRISTMAS WITH AN ALIEN! If you enjoyed this book and want to read more about the Drexians and their tribute bride program, be sure to check out my Tribute Brides of the Drexian Warriors series and the first book (in which you meet Commander Dorn), TAMED!

"I absolutely loved this series... Definitely recommend...but be prepared. I had lots of late nights because I keep saying "only 1 more chapter"!—Amazon Reviewer

For more sexy aliens, one-click TAMED!

* * *

This book has been edited and proofed, but typos are like little gremlins that like to sneak in when we're not looking. If you spot a typo, please report it to: tana@tanastone.com
Thank you!!

ALSO BY TANA STONE

The Tribute Brides of the Drexian Warriors Series:

TAMED (also available in AUDIO)

SEIZED (also available in AUDIO)

EXPOSED (also available in AUDIO)

RANSOMED (also available in AUDIO)

FORBIDDEN (also available in AUDIO)

BOUND (also available in AUDIO)

JINGLED (A Holiday Novella) (also in AUDIO)

CRAVED (also available in AUDIO)

STOLEN (also available in AUDIO)

SCARRED (also available in AUDIO)

ALIEN & MONSTER ONE-SHOTS:

ROGUE (also available in AUDIO)

VIXIN: STRANDED WITH AN ALIEN

SLIPPERY WHEN YETI

CHRISTMAS WITH AN ALIEN

YOOL

Raider Warlords of the Vandar Series:

POSSESSED (also available in AUDIO)

PLUNDERED (also available in AUDIO)

PILLAGED (also available in AUDIO)

PURSUED (also available in AUDIO)

PUNISHED (also available on AUDIO)

PROVOKED (also available in AUDIO)

PRODIGAL

PRISONER

PROTECTOR

PRINCE

The Barbarians of the Sand Planet Series:

BOUNTY (also available in AUDIO)

CAPTIVE (also available in AUDIO)

TORMENT (also available on AUDIO)

TRIBUTE (also available as AUDIO)

SAVAGE (also available in AUDIO)

CLAIM (also available on AUDIO)

CHERISH: A Holiday Baby Short (also available on AUDIO)

PRIZE

SECRET

RESCUE (appearing first in PETS IN SPACE #8)

Inferno Force of the Drexian Warriors:

IGNITE (also available on AUDIO)

SCORCH (also available on AUDIO)

BURN (also available on AUDIO)

BLAZE (also available on AUDIO)

FLAME (also available on AUDIO)

COMBUST

THE SKY CLAN OF THE TAORI:

SUBMIT (also available in AUDIO)

STALK (also available on AUDIO)

SEDUCE (also available on AUDIO)

SUBDUE

STORM

All the TANA STONE books available as audiobooks!
INFERNO FORCE OF THE DREXIAN WARRIORS:

IGNITE on AUDIBLE

SCORCH on AUDIBLE

BURN on AUDIBLE

BLAZE on AUDIBLE

FLAME on AUDIBLE

RAIDER WARLORDS OF THE VANDAR:

POSSESSED on AUDIBLE

PLUNDERED on AUDIBLE

PILLAGED on AUDIBLE

PURSUED on AUDIBLE

PUNISHED on AUDIBLE

PROVOKED on AUDIBLE

BARBARIANS OF THE SAND PLANET

BOUNTY on AUDIBLE

CAPTIVE on AUDIBLE

TORMENT on AUDIBLE

TRIBUTE on AUDIBLE

SAVAGE on AUDIBLE

CLAIM on AUDIBLE

CHERISH on AUDIBLE

TRIBUTE BRIDES OF THE DREXIAN WARRIORS

TAMED on AUDIBLE

SEIZED on AUDIBLE

EXPOSED on AUDIBLE

RANSOMED on AUDIBLE

FORBIDDEN on AUDIBLE

BOUND on AUDIBLE

JINGLED on AUDIBLE

CRAVED on AUDIBLE

STOLEN on AUDIBLE

SCARRED on AUDIBLE

SKY CLAN OF THE TAORI

SUBMIT on AUDIBLE

STALK on AUDIBLE

SEDUCE on AUDIBLE

ABOUT THE AUTHOR

Tana Stone is a USA Today bestselling sci-fi romance author who loves sexy aliens and independent heroines. Her favorite super-hero is Thor (with Aquaman a close second because, well, Jason Momoa), her favorite dessert is key lime pie (okay, fine, *all* pie), and she loves Star Wars and Star Trek equally. She still laments the loss of *Firefly*.

She has one husband, two teenagers, two excitable dogs, and three neurotic cats. She sometimes wishes she could teleport to a holographic space station like the one in her tribute brides series (or maybe vacation at the oasis with the sand planet barbarians). :-)

She loves hearing from readers! Email her any questions or comments at tana@tanastone.com.

Want to hang out with Tana in her private Facebook group? Join on all the fun at: https://www.facebook.com/groups/tanastonestributes/

Made in United States
Troutdale, OR
12/07/2023

15486765R00119